I0614796

# ATTACKING THE ZONE

## SIERRA HOCKEY #5

## ELISE FABER

ATTACKING THE ZONE
BY ELISE FABER

Newsletter sign-up

This is a work of fiction. Names, places, characters, and events are fictitious in every regard. Any similarities to actual events and persons, living or dead, are purely coincidental. Any trademarks, service marks, product names, or named features are assumed to be the property of their respective owners, and are used only for reference. There is no implied endorsement if any of these terms are used. Except for review purposes, the reproduction of this book in whole or part, electronically or mechanically, constitutes a copyright violation.

ATTACKING THE ZONE
Copyright © 2025 Elise Faber
Print ISBN-13: 978-1-63749-179-9
Ebook ISBN-13: 978-1-63749-178-2

# PROLOGUE

## COLT

I CROUCH and unscrew the little black cap, press the tip of the ballpoint pen against the valve.

Air hisses out in a rush.

The tire slowly goes flat.

Is this a crime? Probably.

Is this the first time I've done this? Nope.

Kylie Connors is probably wondering why in the fuck she gets so many flat tires. And I'm the answer. Because every time she ends up with a flat—and this will be the fifth—I'm there to fix it for her.

Because it's the only time she'll acknowledge my presence.

Not when she tags along to team events. Not when we come across each other in the halls of the practice rink or the Sierra's home arena. Not after games or before practice or if we happen to run into each other in town.

It's only when she's trapped on the side of the dark, quiet road that she'll talk to me.

*Look* at me.

And what she gives me during those short moments...it's fucking beautiful. She's funny and smart and—

Intoxicating.

*Irresistible.*

Still, I've tried. To give her space, to let her come to me if and when she decides. To not push even though every part of me demands it.

I know what she went through, know it still haunts her.

So, I waited.

I just...can't any longer.

Because if she's the line I can't cross, I'm already on the wrong side.

I pull the tip of the pen out, survey my handiwork—low enough she shouldn't immediately notice, but enough air gone that she won't make it far.

Perfect. I screw on the cap, slink away to my car, and climb in.

Then I sit and wait for her to walk out of the arena.

To climb into her own car, start up the engine.

And when she drives out of the lot...

I follow.

Because I'm done waiting for Kylie Connors to come to me.

Tonight, everything changes.

# ONE

## KYLIE

"SIIIIX. *SEVEN.*"

I bite back my groan at the nonsense statement that has inundated my classroom for the last few months, having long given up on trying to distract and divert...and understand the intricacies of seventh graders' minds.

This too will pass.

But why does history—and the time period of history I teach in particular (Constantinople to discovering new continents, and all the interesting things in between) have so many sixes?

I go on through the giggles, focusing on the lesson.

It's Story Time.

Because instead of reciting facts and having my students summarize PowerPoint slides, fill in the blanks on handouts with dates they'll never remember, I try to weave history into an exciting story with villains and heroes and plenty of intrigue (and a dash of love for those with romantic souls—namely me).

Thankfully, history provides plenty of fodder for my stories.

And, also thankfully, my fellow teachers in the department are all as enthusiastic as I am about transforming history from the lame, boring subject that was my middle and high school years into something far more interesting.

It took until college for me to discover how multi-faceted, how captivating, how much history impacts our present...

In more ways than one.

But I'm not thinking about my personal history, filled with one of the worst of villains and a morally gray hero (at least on the surface, because my brother, *my* hero, has never been anything but pure).

I'm thinking about Troy.

A story that's fictional yet fits in perfectly with the time period I'm teaching—beautiful, sorrowful—and yes—*romantic*.

So, I focus and get down to Story Time.

Though, while I do it, I try my best to avoid all mentions of sixes...

And sevens.

---

"WHAT TIME ARE YOU COMING OVER?" my brother, Damon, asks, his confident—and finally after all the years of darkness, *happy*—voice coming through the speakers of my car as I navigate the twisting roads.

Pine trees rise up on either side of me, and soon enough snow will cover the ground, hiding the fallen and dried-brown needles.

Skiers and snowboarders will descend—or maybe *ascend*, driving up from the Bay Area, whiling away their time on the slopes.

And the traffic.

Well, that will be hell.

But it's the price I pay for living in paradise.

And the clear air, the beautiful, deep blue lake, the snow and the trees and the valley surrounded by imposing granite mountains is my definition of paradise.

The beach is nice—though, sand getting in *all* the places is not my idea of a good time.

A bustling European city is a great change of pace—if I ignore the traffic and noise and *people*.

It's just that...Tahoe feeds my soul.

No therapy has been better for me than walking along the quiet trails, sitting by the lake, its cold but gentle waves lapping at my toes, standing on the balcony at my apartment or in Damon's back yard, staring up at the sky, seeing so many stars it's like someone has thrown a bag of glitter into the heavens.

But all that beauty doesn't hold a candle to the love I have for my brother.

Even when he's being an overprotective lug.

"I told you," I say as I drive by a turnout on the road, one I've had to stop at several times over the last year because I seem to get an inordinate amount of flat tires, "that I'm not coming over tonight. Enjoy your free evening with Joey—they don't come around all that often during the season."

Because my brother is a former professional hockey player —*former* because he gave it up to protect me—and the current General Manager for the Sierra Hockey organization.

And Joey, his woman, the love of his life, and his fiancée, is the head coach for the team.

For ten months of the year they live and breathe hockey, and since we're in those ten months, the season underway, nights off don't come around all that often.

"They don't," he says, "but I haven't seen you since last week, kid. I need my Kylie fix."

God, I love my big brother.

"I'll come to the game tomorrow," I offer as I turn into my apartment complex. "Tonight, I need a bath and to binge bad TV."

"Kylie," he says gently.

"What?"

"I don't think you should be alone today." It's still gentle, but it's enough to trigger my memory, my recollection of what today's date is.

My stomach churns, hands clenching on the steering wheel, a knot of emotion clogging my throat.

Thankfully, I'm pulling into my parking spot and not driving along the twisting two-lane road because it's all I can do to brake and put the transmission into park.

Then breathe until I can say, "My students have done my head in today."

"Yeah they'll do that," he says lightly before his tone softens, "but you know you don't have to pretend with me, kid."

"I know," I whisper. "Which means I know you'll believe me when I tell you that I didn't remember what day it was until you reminded me."

It's true.

My past is never far away.

But not once had it occurred to me what date today was... and what it changed in me.

He's quiet. Then his curse turns the air blue. "Ky," he says when he's finished, "I'm—"

"Don't." I force my hands to relax on the steering wheel. "You gave me that peace, big bro. Let's take that win."

More quiet. Then a sigh. "I love you."

"Ugh," I groan.

"What'd I do now, kid?"

"You're all happy and in love and in touch with your emotions and shit. It's freaking adorable."

His chuckle soothes the rough edges of the past. "This is something to complain about?"

"Yup," I say. "Little sis privileges."

He laughs again and I know that he'll let it go, let me go and have the night I said I wanted...but I also know that he needs me beside him tonight, needs to know I'm safe and healed and living my life.

And if there's anything *I* need, it's to help him heal his wounds right back.

To be useful.

To be *needed* right back.

Not a burden, not an object to be looked after, but a real functioning human.

I spent too long being the opposite.

"What are you cooking?" I ask.

"Pizza," he says after a moment.

"Barbecue chicken?"

"With olives." His voice is filled with an affection that cups itself around my heart. Yup. I seriously love my big brother. Especially when he adds, "because my freak of a sister likes the disgusting black circles."

"Damon," I say with false affront. "They're not disgusting. They're deliciousness in a tiny mouthful."

"Lies."

"Just because you don't have a sophisticated palate..."

"Is that what we're calling your consumption of copious processed snacks and champagne now?"

"Don't forget popcorn." I slurp. "With extra butter."

He laughs again and I can almost see him shaking his head.

"Damon?"

"Yeah, kid?"

"I'll be over in twenty."

Then I shift the car into reverse...and ignore that the past lurking is at the edges of my mind, just waiting for my defenses to falter.

Same as I ignore that it'll never truly go away.

# TWO

## COLT

"SIIIIX. *SEVEN.*"

Lake Jordan, the captain of the Sierra, curses from where he sits next to me. "It's come for us."

His reply is almost drowned out by the sound of the rookies who've joined the roster for this season bursting into laughter.

"I don't understand kids these days," I mutter.

"Tell me about it." He bumps my skate with his. "We're getting old."

"Old*er*, maybe."

Lake is at the prime of his career—with the points to prove it. He's strong and fast, an incredible goal-scorer and my first emotion upon learning that I was traded to the Sierra was relief.

That I wouldn't have to chase Lake around the ice any longer.

He flashes me a grin that's graced many a billboard and magazine ad. "I knew I liked you."

"But *I'm* still your favorite, right?" Knox says.

"Depends." Lake starts taping his socks.

"On what?"

"Whether Evie is going to say the same shit at Game Night next week."

Knox's step daughter is in second grade and a total spitfire... kind of like his wife, Ivy. The Sierra's strength coach is as fiery as her bright red hair and kicks our ass in the weight room on the regular.

Hell, I know my quads will never be the same.

Knox winces as he tugs on his jock. "Unfortunately, Evie has fully embraced meme culture."

"Christ," Riggs, our taciturn teammate and killer at the blue line, says.

One word.

But it's enough to capture the emotion of the moment.

"I think I'm too old to understand what meme culture is," I mutter.

"We're *definitely* too old for that," Lake says, though his eyes slide to the other side of me, where Storm is sitting.

I know exactly why.

Normally, the younger player would jump on the chance to give us shit, especially when such a softball like us all being a few years older than him was lobbed in his direction.

*Decrepit. Gray hairs coming in. Is that a wrinkle?*

Yeah, it's almost too easy.

But—like he has far too often over the last months—Storm is silent...one might say *stormy*. The cloud of his anger constant and pitch black.

He's talented, but struggling this season, and I know it's because of the woman who's just walked into the room.

Josephine—or, as she's more commonly known—Coach Joey.

Storm fell hard for her.

And she...fell hard for Damon.

Fuck, but I feel for Storm. Sure, there are plenty of single guys on the roster for him to relate with—myself included—but it's one thing to be single by choice and another to be single because the woman you want picked someone else.

Then to have to see that woman almost every day...

To have to work with her...

To have to watch her fall deeper and deeper in love with a man who isn't you...

He's spiraling.

And, based on the parade of women leaving his hotel rooms when we're on the road, he's been doing his best to fuck away his feelings.

I'm clearly not the only one who sees it isn't working.

Lake's gaze comes back to mine and he shakes his head slightly. I know he's watching out for Storm too, same as Knox and Riggs are. We're a team, but we're a team that's been through hell, so we're not going to let him suffer alone.

But an intervention isn't going to happen today.

He's not ready.

Instead, tonight we're going to play some fucking hockey—score some goals, make some plays, dish out some hits, maybe get into some fights, and—

Soft laughter drifts through the open locker room door and...

Yeah, more importantly.

We're going to *win*.

Because Kylie is watching tonight.

Kylie Connors, little sister of Damon Connors, general manager of the Sierra and the man who can make my life miserable here on the Sierra.

By all accounts, she should be off-limits.

But her laughter...*fuck.*

The first time I heard it, swear to God, it felt like phantom fingers wrapped themselves around my heart and squeezed hard.

And haven't let go since.

Every time her pretty blue eyes come to mine my pulse speeds. Every smile she gives me is like fucking poetry and sunshine, a gift I shouldn't accept but can't turn down. And don't get me started on actually being *responsible* for her laughter.

If her smile is poetry, her laughter is...

Beauty personified.

She's not shy—at least not around anyone aside from me. Something I can't decide if I love or hate. Is she scared of me?

The man who raped her was her brother's teammate.

Damon might not be playing any longer but, for all intents and purposes, I occupy the same position as that monster.

So if that reserve was because she was scared of me...well, I would fucking *hate* that.

But maybe, my mind whispers, my soul hopes, *maybe* she's shy with me because of something else.

Maybe it's the same *something* that's drawn me to her.

A connection, a thread of hyperawareness, a need prodding at me to seek out her attention, her smiles and laughter, her... touch.

*That* I would love.

Unfortunately, months into trying to ferret out the answer to the question of Kylie's feelings about me, and I'm no closer to the answer.

Or her touch.

Something that has me wanting to get to my feet and go out into the hall, to trail the soft threads of her laughter through the winding corridors, to draw her close and taste the lush curves of her mouth...

And likely put me and my future career into the crosshairs of her big brother.

Yeah.

I don't want to die today.

I need more time to puzzle out the mystery that's Kylie Connors.

So, I keep my ass firmly on the bench as I finish getting ready for the game—tying my skates with precise movements (finger-tight on the tops of my feet, snug through the bottoms of my ankle, loose on the last eyelet for maximum speed and flexibility). And I stay there as I redo the tape on my stick, as the starting lineup is announced, as I pull on my shoulder pads, strap on my elbow pads, tug on my jersey.

I'm just about to slap my helmet on my head when my cell buzzes.

I reach up, snag my phone.

And grin.

> Blake: I better not see you slacking tonight.

My grin widens and I send my brother a middle finger emoji.

> Blake: I mean it. I've seen your stats, bro.

Shit-giving.

Always.

But something settles in me as I shove my phone away, stand up and follow the guys out into the hall.

I fucking love my younger brother, annoying little shit that he is.

And he's watching too.

So yeah, we're going to fucking *win*.

# THREE

## KY

"WHERE ARE YOU GOING?" Damon asks.

"When are you and Joey going to have a kid?" I counter as I turn back from where I'd been sneaking out of the suite.

He freezes, something like fear in the tense lines of his body, in his jaw as he turns and levels a glare over his shoulder at me. "Seriously, Ky?"

"What?"

"I'm working."

"No, you're glaring out at the ice."

His scowl deepens.

"Okay at me, *and* at the ice."

Narrowed blue eyes, the color a mirror of my own.

Sighing, I abandon my quest for arena popcorn (they always put extra butter on it which makes it de-*lish*-us) and move back to my brother. His gaze is back on the rink below, the players going through the motions of their various warm-up activities.

"I know you want to knock up that gorgeous woman of yours," I say softly, knowing this is the wrong time to be pushing him on this.

But it's also not the first time in the last few months I've seen this reaction from him.

And I'm done waiting for him to either get his head together or talk to me or Joey about it.

I'm going to help him work through his demons the same way he helped me work through mine.

*Yeah? Well what about the demons that keep you up night after night?*

The ones I do my best to pretend don't exist?

Right.

I'm still pretending...that they don't exist.

But also, more important than the crap swirling through my brain, is...what the hell is my amazing big brother thinking?

His expression shouldn't be filled with fear—though, that's tempered by longing. He should be looking forward to the next stage of life, should be moving forward, not clinging to the past.

*Yeah? Like you?*

I clench my teeth together.

Yes. Like *me*.

Moving forward. Not looking back. *Ever.*

Even when the past keeps sinking its claws into me and threatening to yank me off my feet.

"Damon," I press when he doesn't answer.

"We're doing this now?" he mutters.

"When have you ever known me to let something go when it's in my crosshairs?"

A flash of blue eyes. "You're annoying."

"Yeah? Likewise." I nudge his knee with mine. "Talk to me."

"I can't imagine a life without Joey and me starting a family." A shake of his head. "But...it's not the right time."

That's certainly true.

But then there's the fear.

Even masked by calm logic, I can sense his anxiety.

And something in me goes tender as I put the pieces together.

My brother, the one who sacrificed everything for me, is scared of being a good dad.

I want to hug him, put him at ease...and I also want to throttle him.

Because what the fuck?

"You know I was just teasing you about making babies, right?" I pretend to gag, knowing I'll have to go at this sideways to get the stubborn lug to truly absorb what I'm saying. "I don't actually want to think about my brother participating in the act of making *said* babies." When he doesn't unstick, I give him a wet willy.

"*Ky*," he growls, smacking my hand away. "You're not cute."

I smile cherubically. "I absolutely am."

"Are not."

It's tempting to reply *Are so!* But I have more important things to get through his thick skull.

"Big bro." I gentle my voice, know he clocks it because his scowl intensifies, but I push on anyway. "You're going to be a great father—whenever you guys choose to have kids."

"Right," he says gruffly, gaze fixed in place.

I bump his shoulder with mine then sigh again when he doesn't look at me. "You do realize that you were more of a dad to me than our bio dad ever was?"

He sniffs. "Not hard to do considering he left to get milk and never came back."

"I thought it was cigarettes."

"Nah, it was beer."

I relax as we fall into a conversation we've had a hundred times—maybe it trends too much toward dark humor, but sometimes dark humor is the only thing we have to get through the seriously shit times. "Be a better story if he went out to fight aliens or something," I quip. "At least we could say we have a hero for a dad instead of a deadbeat."

The half of Damon's mouth I can see curves up.

Then he exhales and turns toward me, tugging at a lock of my hair that's fallen free of my ponytail.

Not surprising considering it never seems to stay where I want it.

"Tough day in the classroom, huh?" he murmurs.

I lift a shoulder, drop it and know I've battled his stubbornness as much as he'll let me...at least for today. "Eh. You know teenagers. They seem to do their best work by keeping me on my toes."

"That's true enough." He nods toward the door. "Popcorn?"

"Why'd you ask earlier if you already knew where I was going?"

"Because it makes you crazy."

"Who's the annoying one now?" Grinning, I kiss him on the cheek and then, because the tension's left him, I push to my feet.

He picks up his tablet, opens the notes app in preparation for his work during the game. "Hey, kid?"

I still, lift my brows in question.

"Why'd *you* ask about babies if you already knew I was worried about them?"

"Because sometimes I get to fix things too." I pause. "And

because I saw the look on your face when Riggs and Ella announced they were pregnant last week." Bending, I put my lips to his ear. "You want it. And you'll be fucking great at it."

He stills, hands clenching on the tablet. "*Kylie.*"

"And also maybe...because it makes you crazy too." I grin as he scowls again. "I love you, big bro."

Leaving it there, I slip from the suite, make my way through the concourse teaming with people, taking my time as I watch the families and couples, the friend groups and the occasional gathering of work colleagues. It's a cacophony of people and noise and sensation, one that begins to quiet down as I snag my haul of delicious buttery-ness and make my way back, the first bars of the national anthem ringing through the arena.

I wait until the lights come up to drop back down into my seat, the announcer calling out the Sierra's starting lineup.

They're all familiar names—Bear and Riggs at defense, Knox at right wing, Lake at center—

"And at left wing...Colt Madden!"

Colt.

Gorgeous. Nice. A little quiet, though not as taciturn as Riggs.

And the only man I've met in years who makes my pulse speed, my stomach fill with butterflies.

Because...he looks at me.

Like a woman.

Not as a little sister, not as *Damon's* little sister.

But as Kylie Connors.

As something he wants.

Which is...terrifying.

Maybe only slightly *less* terrifying than the fact that I would look at him exactly the same way—

If I wasn't so damned scared.

Because if there's one thing I want most in the world...
It's to give in to my *want* for Colt.
But if there's one thing I know...
It's that will never happen.

# FOUR

## COLT

A GOAL, an assist, and a win all while hyperaware of the woman watching—hopefully—from above.

Then press and working my way through my cooldown routine.

A check in with the training staff.

My post-game meal of chocolate milk and a slice of pepperoni pizza with hot honey.

(A man has needs and oftentimes those needs are fulfilled with pizza topped with hot honey).

But, pizza or not, nothing is as good as the soft laughter fluttering through the hallways.

My footsteps slow, gaze drifting to the right and clinging to Kylie's face.

Her smile...fuck, but it's beautiful.

Then my eyes skate down her body and fuck, but that's beautiful too.

Curved exactly as I like—breasts that will overflow my hands, hips that lead to a lush ass I want to kiss and stroke and bite.

I've fantasized about her so damned much I can picture it.

How I'll stroke her. How I'll kiss her.

How I'll *fuck* her.

If I can ever get her to really look at me, talk to me, *touch* me.

If she's not scared of me.

If she sees me—

Damon's phone rings and he looks down with a curse, hand shoving into his pocket. He scowls when he pulls it out and looks at the screen, says something to Kylie. She nods and then he's gone, disappearing around the corner.

Leaving us alone in the hallway.

Not that she's noticed me.

Except, even as that thought crosses my brain, her head comes up, eyes connecting with mine.

*Hey, gorgeous.*

She jerks, as though she's heard those words sliding through my mind, her gaze tearing away from mine, her shoulders hunching up.

Tense.

Nervous.

Of me? Or of what she feels?

Maybe I should turn around, finish getting changed, and go home to my empty house.

But I don't.

Instead, I move carefully down the hall, stopping a couple of feet away, leaning back on the opposite wall.

Giving her plenty of space to escape.

But, God, I hope she doesn't want to.

"Hey," I say when she doesn't look at me.

A flash of blue eyes that are so fucking beautiful they take my breath away. "Hey," she murmurs back.

And...silence.

A million things pass through my mind in an instant—questions to ask, statements to break the quiet that's fallen between us, poetry to recite—and instead, what comes out is...

"Do you like hot dogs?"

Okay.

Seriously. What the *fuck*, Madden?

This is charming?

It's fucking inane.

Kylie goes still.

Then her head lifts again, tilting slightly to the side as her eyes come back to mine...and hold.

And inane or not, the blurted-out question gives me this—

A glimpse of the bright, mischievous woman beneath the shy.

"Hot dogs?" she asks, eyes sparkling.

I feel like the biggest idiot on the planet...and also like I'm hoisting the Cup again.

At the same time.

"Yeah," I say, doubling down because at this point I have no choice *but* to double down. "Hot dogs."

Her lips twitch. "I've been around locker rooms far too much to take that bait, Colt."

I grin. "Yeah?"

"Yes." A beat. "Definitely."

"Well, maybe it was just an innocent question about the only meal I know how to cook," I counter.

"Liar."

I lift my eyebrows.

"You made lasagna the last time you hosted Game Night."

"I didn't think you ate any."

It had been the first and only time I hosted—mostly because Kylie had come but had seemed so uncomfortable in my space, I made it so I wasn't free to host since.

(Turns out my house has a lot of leaks. And termites. And appliances breaking down.)

"It was so good I snuck an extra slice into a Tupperware I had in my purse."

"You carry Tupperware in your purse?"

A delicate shoulder lifts and falls in a shrug and she giggles. "Maybe."

Beautiful.

So fucking beautiful.

Then she pushes off the wall.

I hold my breath as she comes close.

Five feet away. Three. *One.*

Her hand lifts toward my face and still, I don't breathe, don't speak, don't dare to move as her fingertips come closer.

Closer.

*Touch.*

Everything inside me lights up—joy and yearning and feeling alive for the first time in a long time...maybe the first time ever.

Because Kylie is touching me.

Her hand skates over my jaw, fingers gently trailing along the stubble there, and—

She pulls back, pointer finger and thumb pinched together.

"I don't think glitter goes with your outfit," she teases, holding up the sparkling speck.

My heart is pounding like I've just sprinted across the ice, trying desperately to catch up with some fucker on the other team. "Must have been from the kids earlier."

She brushes her hand on her pants, leaving that speck there, and though I'm tempted—so *fucking* tempted—to touch her with the excuse of removing that fleck from her jeans—I remain in place. "I met them with Damon," she says softly. "They were adorable."

I think of the kids with their beanies and face paint (and glitter), and grin.

"Yeah, they were definitely that."

*Like someone else I know.*

Her eyes flare and I know I've given away too much.

"Well," she whispers, stepping back. "I'm sure you're tired." Her gaze slides away, shy creeping back up and over her. "I'll let you get out of here."

I reach forward and snag her wrist, staying her when she would have walked away. "Kylie."

Blue eyes on mine. Lips parting on a shaky exhale. Her body drifts toward mine and for one hopeful heartbeat, I think this might be the moment.

But it's gone a heartbeat later, lost in Damon's terse "Goodbye," that echoes around the corner, in reality intruding on this moment.

When she tugs at my hold, I immediately let her go.

Never do I want to see fear in those gorgeous eyes when she looks at me.

"Goodnight, Colt," she murmurs.

"Night, Kylie," I murmur back, watching as she starts down the hall, soaking up the sight of her face when she glances back over her shoulder at me.

Because there's warmth there.

And hope.

And maybe, just fucking *maybe*, the barest hint of the same need I feel when I look at *her*.

And maybe that need is why I slip out into the parking lot, crouch near her car, and slowly let the air out of her tire again.

Or maybe I do it for a totally different reason altogether.

One that means...

Everything is going to change.

# FIVE

## KY

I TWIST the knob and turn up the song, listening to John Fogerty sing about rain on a sunny day.

It's beautiful and simple, promising me that the storm will pass and beauty will come in its place.

Though, I can't help but think of the song's original meaning.

Of an impending storm, of conflict battling with joy, of ties fracturing.

My body ping-pongs between those two sensations—hope and terror, fear to step out of the shadows and a yearning to move forward. To be free. To find solace in the rainbows that come after the storm.

I just don't know what side I'll land on.

Standing in the rain, chilled through to the bone.

Or the water on my skin unnoticed because the rainbows are all I see.

The sounds of the guitar fade and I get ready for my playlist to throw something else at me—it could be anything from more seventies rock to a popular ballad inundating my social feeds, talking about being the man I need. Or eighties hair bands. Or nineties alt rock. Or current R&B divas.

It has a good beat and lyrics I can get lost in?

I'm down.

Because I love music—the escape it gives me, the stories I can live without leaving my house, my car, my—

"Oh no," I whisper when the chime goes.

My eyes flick to the dash, to the little light that's appeared on the screen.

A light I've seen far too often over the last months.

I turn the corner, pull into the turnout. *Our* turnout.

And I wait.

Not long—not long at all—for the headlights to flash in my rearview, for the car to pull to a stop behind me.

I wait until I'm sure it's him before I open my door and climb out.

Normally, I wait for him to speak, to approach, to bridge the gap, ease the edges of my fear so I can talk to him without feeling like an idiot...or like a woman.

One of those is scarier than the other.

Any guesses which?

Because the thought of being a woman again—not a little sister, not a friend, not a teacher...a *woman*.

That's scary, a role I haven't been able to accept.

But something changed tonight.

Maybe it's that I'm tired, that I don't want to be here on the side of the road.

Maybe it's that I touched him.

My pulse speeds at the memory of how the roughness of the bristles on his jaw felt on my fingertips, how the heat in his eyes both rubbed over my skin like sandpaper and set every nerve on fire, making me yearn for so much more.

How, for a second there, I *was* a woman again.

So maybe...it's that I walked away from him hoping I would find myself in this exact spot.

With him.

Not knowing—okay, or maybe not wanting to *accept*—which is the truth has me forgetting to be nervous.

I plunk my hands on my hips and scowl at Colt as he walks over to me. "I'm not stupid, you know."

His steps hitch but he recovers quickly. "Car trouble?" he asks, ignoring the assertion.

Or at least I think he's going to.

But instead of going to the trunk, waiting for me to pop it because he knows *exactly* where I keep my spare tire, he pauses a couple of feet away. "And I don't think you're stupid, baby."

Heat and fear.

Need and terror.

He doesn't touch me, doesn't box me in.

But he does keep looking at me and here, under the star-filled sky, the safety of the shadows, the quiet of the darkened world, I find I can look at him right back. At least until something ripples through his expression, a devastation that's so complete, so vast, it feels like a knife has been plunged into my stomach and yanked up, tearing me wide open.

Or maybe that's his quiet words.

"You're scared of me."

Not a question.

A fact.

"Yes."

More devastation that wounds me as much as I've just wounded him.

"I would never hurt you."

My throat gets tight. "I know."

He takes a step toward me then immediately freezes. "Then why?" he rasps.

I should lie.

But I can't, not here, not in our place. "Because I'm scared of what you make me feel."

His eyes close.

Another should—as in I should leave it there, leave it alone.

Let this fade away.

If I asked, I know Colt would disappear from my life.

I just...part of me can't let him go.

"You played well tonight," I murmur.

His eyes fly open and the warmth in them, even partially hidden by the night is...about the furthest thing from scary as I've ever experienced. "Thanks."

We stand there for a moment, gazes locked.

Then I blurt, "Hot dogs?"

He starts and I swear if it wasn't so dark, I think I would have seen his cheeks going red. "There's a new place in town," he says as he moves to the back of my car and opens the hatch. "I thought we could try it."

I still.

I see that *he's* gone still.

Then I breathe.

*Live.*

"If I agree to try it will you stop with the tires?"

He straightens so quickly he hits his head on the open trunk. "Fuck," he mutters, shifting out from beneath it. "What did you say?"

I just lift my brows. "Tires, Colt." Then add when his face goes blank, "Like I said, I'm not stupid."

He's still, but only for a moment.

Then he comes close again, slow and steady...and still not blocking my exit route.

Maybe that care should make me mad—wasn't I just thinking I don't want to be a burden, an object to be looked after? I certainly don't want this man to see me as a fragile, limp dishrag of a human.

But...I'm not mad.

Instead, I'm...*touched.*

That he's looked closely enough to see through my walls, to understand that, though I may *want* to be free of my past, it lingers.

And so, he takes care with me.

So yeah, not mad. *Touched.*

And it gives me the strength to move closer.

Near enough to feel the heat of his body, to smell the spicy hint of his cologne, to see the small scar he has beneath his bottom lip.

To search his eyes and find no hint of a monster within.

"Like I said," he murmurs, staying in place as I get close, as I find myself lifting my hand to his face again, brushing my fingers along his jaw.

Even raspier than before.

Stubble that won't take much to turn into a full beard.

"Like you said what?" I press when he doesn't go on.

"You're not stupid."

He shifts, just slightly, bending so he's leaning into my touch, and it's not fear I'm feeling.

Our bodies are close, but our lips even closer.

If I rose on tiptoe, just an inch, maybe two, I could kiss him.

And that...

I find that I want *that* a lot.

But even as I'm working up the courage to do precisely *that,* he turns his head, lips gliding *oh so lightly* over my palm.

I gasp, but he's slipping away, going back to the trunk, and pulling out my spare.

In less than a minute, he's positioning the jack. "Kylie?" he calls.

I shake myself. "Yeah?"

"What's going on with that show of yours?"

My lips twitch. "The best show in the history of all shows?"

He laughs as he starts cranking, lifting the car, drawing my focus to his strength, his competence. "If you say so."

"I think *you* said so, considering you asked about it."

"I'll neither confirm or deny," he says as he loosens the lug nuts and makes short work of changing the tire.

But as he falls quiet, I fill the silence.

With talk about the awesome show.

And more.

Because when he asks, I tell him about my terrible crochet projects (I'm working on a turtle that looks very much...*not* like a turtle), about my kids and the shenanigans they get up to, about the new games Damon and Joey want to try out next Game Night, about the little hiking trail near my apartment where I like to clear my mind.

Eventually, he finishes with the tire and stores it in the trunk—where I know it will just need air and to be swapped back out for the spare.

Then he comes back over to me, mouth hitched up on one side. "All set."

"No more tires," I murmur.

His half smile turns into a full...and it's so beautiful my heart skips a beat. "Goodnight, Kylie," he murmurs back before getting into his car.

But he doesn't drive away.

And I know it's because he's waiting for me to go first.

Same as I know he'll follow me all the way back to my apartment and watch until I let myself inside.

I know all that...

But it doesn't occur to me until I'm winding through the darkened roads—

That he didn't promise about the tires.

# SIX

## COLT

"AND THEN I SNIPED HIM, bro. Seriously sniped him."

Blake laughs and I can tell by the way it sounds that he's having a rough day.

Health-wise.

Not mentally.

Blake, for all that my little brother has endured in his life—hospital stays, double-digit surgeries, so fucking many doctors' appointments and procedures and medications—isn't often unwell mentally.

He's the strongest person I know.

And I don't mean that he's just hiding his thoughts and feelings and struggles behind a veneer of fake, toxic positivity.

I mean he was born with a shit hand, can't go out and act like us normal, healthy folk, but he still manages to live a life that's far more complete than the nonsense I've been pretending to live.

On the road half the year.

Living and breathing hockey the rest of it.

Alone when I'm not with the team.

Things have gotten a little better since I was traded to the Sierra—mostly because Knox and Lake and the others make it impossible to keep my distance.

But I'm not exactly living what anyone would call a full life.

Blake, on the other hand, can't leave the house all that often (and even more rarely for something that isn't a doctor's appointment) has a packed social calendar with friends all over the world.

*Call of Duty* with his friends in Berlin.

*Wavelength* with his friends in Australia.

The newest *Roblox* game with his friends in Brazil.

Video games and chatting online keep him sane, but it's not all Blake does. He's on the board of the children's charity I founded when I got my first big contract in the league, he fosters kittens, and he does social media for a variety of brands.

See? A full life.

Certainly more so than me with my sticks and pucks and skates.

"Why were you sniping again?"

He sighs the put-out sigh that only younger siblings can do. "Because he was being a dickhead with Sara."

"And who is Sara?" I can't help but ask, drawing out her name to about ten syllables.

He pauses and I picture him glaring at the phone. Then he sighs again. "You're annoying."

"And *you've* got it bad," I tease.

"Bro—"

"You know I can always get another ticket to the team's celebration," I offer. "And you can impress her with your hockey prowess and behind-the-scenes privileges."

"Yeah, right," he mock grumbles. "Last thing I need is one of those playboys you call teammates catching her eye."

"True. You definitely can't compete with that kind of sex appeal."

Silence.

Then, "You know if you weren't my brother, I'd..."

"Wish you could have my abs?"

He snorts. "God, you're an asshole sometimes," he says, but he's laughing.

"Sure am," I say and I'm laughing too.

I pull to a stop in front of the practice facility and throw the transmission into park. "I'm serious about the extra ticket though."

"I'll ask her." He coughs slightly, and I know it's because of the fluid around his heart. "But she might have to work."

Yup. Maybe it's cliché, but Sara and Blake met in the cafeteria of the hospital.

She's a nurse in one of the departments.

And my brother is charming when he's not giving me shit.

It's a match that means he's fallen hard enough I hope she doesn't break his heart.

Though, she seems just as smitten.

Now if I can just get my mom to unclench enough so Blake can take her on an actual date...

Maybe this event will be that chance, especially since they're all coming out.

"Well, either way," I tell him. "The ticket will be there waiting for her. And her flight would be on me."

"Th—"

"Who may have to work?"

It's a shrill question.

And not from Blake.

"Mom," he begins. "Colt's on the phone—"

"*Who* Blake Madden?" she presses.

"Sara." He sighs when she makes a sharp sound but doesn't back down. "Remember how we're going to the celebration the Sierra are putting on for Colt's five hundredth game in the league? Colt said he could get an extra ticket for Sara."

I can't believe it's been that long.

Can't believe that in all of those games, Blake has only been able to convince our parents (well, really, our mom because our dad is more interested in his phone than anything to do with either of us) to allow him to come to a half-dozen of them.

"A *celebration with the Sierra?!*" she exclaims. "Absolutely not, Blake."

"Mom! You promised!"

"And what if you get sick? There are twenty thousand people at those games!"

"I've already arranged for you guys to have a suite," I interject. "Blake won't have to sit out in the arena."

Silence.

"And none of you have to participate in any of the events if you don't want to. Though Doc is aware of Blake's conditions and took them into account. Most of the events will be outside and the inside ones will have handwashing stations and masks available."

More silence.

Then, "It's too dangerous. You know if your brother picks up a bug, he can get seriously ill. Do you want Blake to get sick?" Her voice blasts through the speakers, hard and accusing. "Do you want him to *die?*"

"Mom," Blake begins, exasperation heavy in his tone. "I'm—"

"You know your doctor advised that you avoid crowds, especially after the last time. Your lungs are scarred from your medications and we're going into flu season."

"So, I'll wear a mask." He coughs, his breaths sounding shallower, faster. "And wash my hands."

Because he's frustrated.

Because he's having a bad day.

"I can't not live my life—" He breaks off, his cough wetter, raspier. "I—" He tries to keep talking, but my mom is talking too, talking over him, all that shrill overpowering him, especially since he's fighting against the coughing, the shortness of breath.

And I can't listen any longer.

Can't be the cause of this shit.

Not again.

"It's fine," I say quietly. Then again, more loudly. "*Mom*," I finally interject sharply, shouting to be heard over her cacophony of words. "It's fine. There are always more games. We'll find one that works better."

"Only if he's careful and not sick and—"

"Enough, Mom," Blake snaps. "I'm going."

"Blake, it's cool," I say.

"It's not," he growls.

A sniff has my stomach clenching, my teeth grinding together. "I just worry about you, is all," our mom says and I know the tears are getting ready to come. *Christ.* "I just love my baby boy."

I absorb that blow as I always do.

The singular *baby boy.*

Because I'm the afterthought.

"Mom—" Blake begins.

"I need to get to the pharmacy and pick up your prescriptions."

"I have them scheduled for delivery—"

"It's always better if I go in person. You know they get it

wrong half the time..." she says, her voice fading as she presumably leaves for the pharmacy.

The quiet falls again.

"C...olt," Blake says and fuck, just hearing him trying to push out my name kills.

"It's good," I tell him. "Promise. We'll find another way to impress Sara."

"I—" he rasps. "You know Mom just—"

I can't do this right now.

"I need to go, bud. It's almost time for practice and I don't want to be late."

"You...know I love...you?"

"Yeah," I say, closing my eyes for a second. "You know I love *you?*" A beat. "Even though you're a fucking pain in the ass?"

"Same, bro. Same." He laughs and it still sounds rough.

But at least the pity is gone from his voice when we say our goodbyes.

# SEVEN

## KY

"AND THE LAST item that we need to address is the topic of Adrian."

I frown, set my notebook down on the edge of Holly desk and brace.

I don't like the principal's tone.

And Adrian is sick—has been sick his whole life but is really struggling this year. He's only been in my class a handful of times in the couple of months school has been in session. The rest of the time he's been at home.

Or in the hospital.

"What's happened?" I ask, tightening my stomach muscles against what impact might be coming my way.

I know that bad things happen to good people—God, how I know that.

But not one of my kids.

He may not have spent a lot of time in my classroom in

person, but he's active in the digital one, a bright ball of joy on our Zoom calls, and truly a pleasure in his emails.

He's just...good.

And I hope to God that Holly isn't about to tell me that his special brand of *good* is leaving this world—

"He's coming back to school."

I straighten, relief shooting through me so rapidly that my eyes start burning.

Blinking to prevent any pesky tears from escaping, I clear my throat and pick up my notebook, start writing as I say, "Okay, so what do we need to facilitate that? Our students are familiar with handwashing and masks, especially post-COVID, but is there anything else that he'll need to be successful?"

The beat of quiet is long enough that my list of things I need to make my classroom safe—and how to get the students on board with supporting them—is finished, the scratching of my pen on the paper subsiding.

Then I'm back to bracing.

"What?" I ask quietly.

"I think we need to continue pushing virtual school as the best option."

I pause, breathe.

But before I can come up with something I want to say (something that won't get me reprimanded...or fired), she continues, "So there's no need to bend over backwards to make a ton of in-person accommodations, especially with the school year well underway."

I pause again.

Breathe. *Again.*

Then say, each word tight and clipped. "I'm not sure I understand what you're saying."

I do.

But I also don't fucking want to believe it.

Because this is not what I thought this school was, not who I thought Holly was.

She sighs and leans back in her chair, the leather creaking in protest, and I'd like to think it's protesting in solidarity with me.

And the bullshit that is swirling in this room.

"You know that funding is down," Holly says, and that's true.

"But it's not a funding issue," I remind her. "It's a legal issue. He has a right to be in the classroom—"

"But he will be in the classroom. The virtual classroom, so legally we're covered."

My temper, quiet and not often prone to eruption—mostly because it's regularly tested by twelve- and thirteen-year-olds— begins to boil up.

In a minute, it's going to be boiling *over*.

"Let's face it," she says. "Yeah, he might be back in the classroom for a couple of weeks, but he's going to get sick again. That's just the fact of life," she adds, volume rising to speak over me when I start to reply. "If we put in all this time and effort and money to accommodate him, what are we taking away from the other students?"

My temple starts to throb.

My temp*er* is contained by the most slender thread of my control.

I grind my teeth together and stand. "I'll coordinate with Adrian's parents about what we need to get him back in the classroom."

Holly opens her mouth.

"Once that's done, I'll let the others"—Adrian's vice princi-pal, the counseling office, the nurse—"know what's needed so we can coordinate."

Holly's lips press flat.

"For now"—I deliberately glance at my phone—"it's getting late and I have to head out."

I gather my stuff, start shoving them into my bag, rage such a tightly coiled ball inside me that it's taking everything to keep it contained.

Breathe.

Calm.

Persist.

But I want to *persist* by smacking her upside the head to knock some sense into her.

Or maybe by going all Jason Bourne and using my pen for some stabby stab.

Since neither are reasonable options, I just throw my purse over my shoulder and stand.

"Kylie," Holly says as I reach the door. "I'm not trying to..."

I wait for her to finish that.

But she can't.

Because she's trying to do exactly what she's pretending not to.

"Bye, Holly," I say and head out of the office, forcing a smile at Tonya, the receptionist, but doing my best to avoid eye contact with anyone else, lest I explode.

It's not until I'm in my car, seatbelt buckled, hands clenched on the steering wheel that I allow myself to release the shriek of frustration.

Then I realize I'm screaming in my car. At my place of work. Where kids—and maybe their parents—are still around, attending club meetings or going to sports practices.

So, I get it together.

I'm good at that—shoving down the feelings, the rage, the hurt, the frustration and angst and sadness.

Once I'm calm, I turn on the ignition, back out of the spot

and carefully navigate my way to the road that leads to my apartment.

I don't bother with music.

I don't want to be soothed.

I want to be angry, to rage, to sit in this injustice.

Tomorrow, I'll come back with a clear head, will problem-solve and be all the things I should be.

But right now, I'm going to brood.

Okay? *Okay.*

That's my right and no one is going to—

*Pop!*

I scream as my car lurches sharply to the side, then react on instinct and wrench at the wheel. It takes every bit of strength I have to not slide off the road, to avoid the boulders and trees as I slam on the brakes and muscle my car—

To the turnout...

To *our* turnout.

But then I've come to a stop.

I sit frozen for a long moment, just breathing, just *existing*.

Then I realize I'm stuck on the freaking turnout with another *freaking* flat tire.

And...fuck it.

That second shriek I'd bitten off back in the parking lot at school?

I let that fucker fly.

Then I drop my forehead to the steering wheel...

And I let the tears come too.

# EIGHT

## COLT

EXHAUSTION PULLS at my limbs as I make the drive home.

Practice was tough, but not anything insane.

Coach wants to make sure we're at the top of our games and well-conditioned, but she doesn't want to burn us out early in the season.

No, we push it in the weight room, on the bikes.

But on the ice we...finesse.

We work hard, we battle and get our heart rates up, but it's the finer details rather than the intense exercise that conditions us for the season.

Still, that doesn't mean I'm not ready to get home, shove some food in my mouth, and pass out.

Only...

It doesn't work out that way.

Because as I turn the corner, thoughts on dinner and my bed, I see a familiar little red SUV on the turnout.

On *our* turnout.

Frowning, I slow and pull to a stop behind Kylie's car.

It's leaning heavily to the side...

The tire blown out.

The irony of the situation slides through my head, but it's quickly chased out by concern as I shove open my door and hurry toward her car. Hers isn't a tire that's low on air. It's one that's in shreds and...

This near to the edge of the road, to the drop-off that's far too close, to the cluster of evergreens and the giant granite boulder—

*Fuck.*

My heart is pounding by the time I reach the driver's side door.

I don't think as I reach for the handle and find it locked.

"Fuck," I whisper. Her hands are clenched on the steering wheel, forehead resting between them, and the engine's still running. I knock on the window, watch as she jumps.

The car drifts forward a couple of feet before she realizes what's happening and slams on the brakes.

"Unlock the door, Kylie," I say loudly enough to be heard through the glass.

There's a pause, her eyes holding mine for a moment.

"Hit the locks, baby."

She jerks, but her hand reaches toward the door and a second later, I hear the locks disengage.

I have the door open and I'm leaning over her, shoving the transmission into park and turning off the engine before I realize that I'm crowding her, that I might be scaring her.

"Fuck, Ky. I'm sorry," I say, maneuvering out and crouching.

Her hands are still clenched on the steering wheel and I'm close enough to see her throat work as she swallows. "I-it's okay," she whispers. "Thanks."

"What happened?"

She finally releases a hand from the steering wheel and shoves it through her hair. I don't miss that it's shaking as it disappears into the long brown strands of her ponytail, and I want to snag it, to wrap my fingers around hers and hold it tight.

But I don't.

"Tire blew," she says a moment later, dropping it into her lap.

But when I watch it clench into a fist I can't stop myself, can't remember why I'm supposed to keep my distance.

So, fuck it, I take her hand, gently lace our fingers together.

"It wasn't me," I blurt.

She jerks but doesn't pull out of my hold.

Nope, her fingers tighten around mine and then she's holding me right back.

Fuck.

That's...

Well, it's almost as good as that stroke of her fingers through my stubble back at the arena.

*Almost.*

Then she laughs and the mental order I've been making of all the good of Kylie Connors is scattered again.

Because *that* tops everything.

"Who are you?" she teases. "Shaggy?"

I snort, but the slice of dry humor referencing the old two thousands song relaxes me enough that I reach up and brush my thumb beneath her eye. "You've been crying."

Not a question because those beautiful blue eyes are reddened and a little swollen, her lashes clinging together from the tears that left faint tracks on her cheeks.

Her exhale is a little shaky but I don't pull back.

Or maybe it's that I can't.

"Why, baby?"

Half of her mouth quirks up and she exhales again, though this time it's not shaky. It's...frustrated. I lurch toward the emotion, hoarding the new piece of her like I'm Gollum and she's the shining gold ring.

Mine. *Mine.*

My precious.

"I had a day," she says ruefully.

"The kids?"

A sigh. "They're always challenging, but they're good kids and that challenge is good, is something that makes the days interesting."

"How?"

"There's routine and yet, they're never the same." She lifts one delicate shoulder in a shrug, lets it fall. "They're never boring."

"I know what you mean," I tell her.

Her head tilts, her ponytail sliding over the back of my hand.

Silk.

God, what I wouldn't give to have the strands spread on my pillow.

"I guess you do." She smiles softly and I take that piece of her too.

Because I'm greedy when it comes to Kylie Connors.

"And I know it wasn't you," she says. "You wouldn't hurt me."

I freeze, fingers flexing on her cheek.

Yup. At this point I'm going to have to make a whole new list of things I love about Kylie.

And number one is going to be the way she can eviscerate me with only four words.

I should say something, should reaffirm, make it clear I'd cut off my arm before I allow harm to come to her.

But she speaks before I can get my head together enough to give voice to that.

"But, for old time's sake"—her lips curve into a smile I've seen her give others, but never me—"would you put your tire changing skills to use for me?"

I'd crawl through a mile of broken glass for her.

But all I say is, "Yeah, baby."

Pink on her cheeks, warming the skin beneath my fingertips, and fuck, I want to lean in, to close the distance between us, to taste those plump lips.

Instead...I pull back.

I need to get her safe, need to get her home, need to find out why her day was a *day* and figure out how to make it better.

Need to figure out how to tell her I'm never letting her go.

But first I *need* to change her tire.

So I get on that.

# NINE

## KY

HE FOLLOWED ME HOME.

Because of course he did.

But now, instead of idling at the curb, watching me climb the stairs to my apartment, he's parked in a guest spot and he's walking toward me, all easy, loose-limbed strength.

If only I ignore the look in his eyes.

Like he's seen something he wants.

Like I'm the prey to his predator and he's begun his hunt.

Maybe, given my past, that should be terrifying.

But I can't ignore the hidden thrill coiling in my belly—nor the notion that to be hunted and caught by this man would mean to be held safely in the protection of him for the rest of my life.

Caught but not caged.

So no, I don't bolt like a gazelle on the savannah.

I freeze...maybe like a gazelle on the savannah.

But maybe also like a woman who's finally ready to grasp on to the future.

"You have dinner plans?" I ask when he's close.

And get to watch the pleased surprise travel through his face. "Yes."

"Oh," I say, disappointment sliding through me. Is it possible I've misread—

A tug on my ponytail. "With you."

Heat on my cheeks...warmth in my belly.

"Want me to order something?" he asks, snagging my bag from my shoulder and walking toward the apartment building, leaving me with no choice but to follow him. "Since you've had a *day?*" he tosses over his shoulder when I get close again, and my breath catches at the sparks of gold in his eyes.

They're beautiful.

Kind of like the man himself.

A man I haven't allowed myself to notice.

Because if I did, I might...

"My day wasn't that bad," I say as we climb the stairs side-by-side.

"It was bad enough to make you cry," he points out and he's not wrong.

"That was more of an adrenaline letdown from nearly skidding off the road," I say dryly.

I expect him to chuckle.

Instead, when he's silent and I look up at him, I find he's scowling.

"What?"

His scowl deepens but he just nods toward my apartment door, silently indicating I unlock it. I input the code, hear the quiet *whir* as it disengages, then twist the handle and push it open.

"What?" I ask again when he just waves a hand, dispatching another silent order—this one for me to go inside.

I only listen because I want to know what's put the scowl on his face.

But at some point (soon), he'll need to cool it on the commands—silent or otherwise.

"That was really dangerous," he grinds out, closing and locking the door behind him.

I feel something in me catch, a flicker of awareness that Colt is the first man I've been alone with in my apartment that isn't my brother, that he's the first man I've been alone with like *this* since I opened the door and let Dylan in all those years before.

Pausing, I wait for the panic to come, to flood through my nerves and overpower my thoughts, my place in the present, yanking me fiercely back into the past.

Instead...

I'm still here.

And now I'm left wondering why Colt has gone so still, so tense.

Curiosity has the knot in my belly loosening and I ask, "What do you mean?"

"The tire blowing, the winding road. Fuck the fucking *trees*." He clamps his teeth together and shakes his head sharply. "What I did was fucking stupid." Blazing brown eyes on mine. "I'm so sorry, Kylie. I wasn't thinking."

Phantom fingers wrap tightly around my heart and squeeze. "Colt," I murmur. "That wasn't your fault."

"How do you know?" he mutters. "I've been fucking with your tires for months and—"

I move toward him, do something else that only Colt seems to unlock—I touch him and don't feel fear.

"It was a brand new tire," I tell him. "After your most

recent...*mischief*"—I slide my hand from his shoulder, back up to his jaw, the spiky bristles of the stubble there grounding me in the now. Or maybe it's just that touching him is addictive— "the tire guys insisted on doing a full workup. I got four new tires." A beat as I grin up at him. "With locking caps."

His eyes come to mine.

Still blazing.

But not in fear and anger.

In...

Something else that I can't name.

Because if I do, if I admit I'm feeling the same thing, I don't think I'll be grounded here in the present.

I'll be right back in the past.

He covers my hand with his own. "You won't need those for me." Gentle bleeding into his eyes as he peels my hand from his cheek. "Not any longer." A kiss to the center of my palm. "Not ever again."

My lungs hitch.

"Now dinner, baby."

Another hitch as his fingers wrap around mine and squeeze. He shoves his free hand into his pocket and I know he's searching for his phone, ready to make good on that promise to order in dinner for us.

"Dinner is in the crockpot," I say, tilting my head toward the kitchen. "I just need to bake off the bread and serve it up."

He sniffs. "Is that the deliciousness I'm smelling?"

I grin. "Does it do something to your hockey street cred to use words like *deliciousness*?"

"Probably." A shrug. "But there's always something to be given shit about, so I don't give a fuck if they tease me about the proper usage of words like *deliciousness*." He winks at me. "Especially when whatever it is that I'm smelling is exactly that."

"What else do the guys give you shit about?" I ask as I move into the kitchen, giving him a silent order—*ha!*—of my own (that being to hang my school bag on its proper hook).

(He does).

"How about I tell you after you tell me why your day was such a *day?*" He moves over to me as I pull the bowls down, snag the ladle from the drawer I keep it in.

"It really isn't that big of a—"

"What temperature do you want the oven at?"

"Wh-what?" I ask, spinning from the sudden change in conversational topic.

"For the bread, what temperature?"

I blink. Then again.

"Never mind," he says, snagging the loaf of grocery store garlic bread. "I can read."

"I—"

He turns to the oven, fiddles with the knobs. "Now, talk to me."

"I—" Then I shake my head. "You're not going to let this go, are you?"

His mouth tips up. "What do you think?"

I *think* that if my brother is stubborn, Colt takes it to the next level.

"Food first," I grumble. "Then I'll complain to you about my boss."

# TEN

## COLT

"AND THEN MY tire blew and I almost hit those trees and..." She shrugs. "You know the rest of it."

My stomach twists again.

Fuck, it could have easily gone so wrong.

The shit I pulled.

All just to get a little more time with her.

She could have—

I clench my teeth together. No more fucking tires.

*Ever.*

Kylie sets her spoon down with a clink and takes my hand. "Stop it," she orders. "I already have one man in my life who worries about me too much."

"What man?" I ask sharply.

*Too* sharply.

But she doesn't cower or pull back.

Instead, she rolls her eyes and picks up her spoon again. "My brother," she says dryly before scooping up a bite of the white chicken chili. "And he's had more practice at being a pain in the ass, so cool it."

"Are you sure?"

"That I want you to cool it?" Her brows flick up and the sass in the blue depths (the evidence that she's getting comfortable with me) sends a thrill through me. "Yes."

"No, baby. Are you sure that he's had more practice being a pain-in-the-ass older brother?" I ask instead of kissing that tart rejoinder off that gorgeous mouth of hers.

"I—" She stops, head tilting to the side. "I guess I *don't* know that." Her head slants the other direction, her ponytail swinging behind her. "Do you have siblings?"

I nod. "A younger brother. Blake."

"How much younger?"

"Six years."

Her mouth kicks up. "I stand corrected. You *do* have plenty of time at being a pain in the ass."

I laugh. "Is this where I should mention my opinion on younger siblings and *their* pain-in-the-assness?"

She laughs and I feel like I'm a fucking superhero, zooming through the air, catching crumbling buildings before they can crush the innocents below.

"Rude," she says when she's done, reaching for her spoon again. "Eat."

"You sure got the bossy younger sister down pat."

She freezes, spoon an inch away from the delicious chili she so casually served me. Then she narrows her eyes in my direction. "You want to think again? Or," she adds before I can continue teasing her, "you want to rephrase that? Perhaps to amend that statement in favor of *all* the bossy older siblings?"

"Nope," I tease.

Laughter in her eyes, in the air. "Incorrigible."

"The dumb hockey player in me doesn't know the meaning of that word."

"Liar," she says as she primly scoops up more chili. "Don't think I've missed the fact that you're never without a book."

I still.

Because I've noticed so much about her—the way she takes her coffee, the wine she likes, how she is still, months later, determinedly trying to learn how to crochet (even though the creations still aren't turning out all that well). I know which of Nova's Moscow mules she prefers, which game she gets competitive over Ella with. I know that she gets irritated at her brother for checking up on her but she does it with a soft look on her face, like she knows it's from love and a need to look after her when, once, he couldn't protect her. I know she did something called a bubble braid for Ivy's daughter, Evie, at the last home game she attended (adding plenty of sparkle) and that she funds a lot of her classroom supplies out of her own pocket.

And I know that she cares about her kids deeply.

Something that was doubly confirmed tonight when her eyes teared up while talking about her student, when frustration colored her words when she spoke about her meeting with the school's principal.

Such bullshit.

But my brother and mother waded through that often enough that I know it—legal or not—happens regularly.

And it means something that Kylie cares—truly cares—about her students.

Enough to fight for them.

To know them.

Yet, even understanding that...hell, I didn't truly think she put any effort into understanding *me*, into knowing me.

Avoiding? Sure.

"What?" she asks.

I shake my head. "I just didn't think that anyone noticed."

Pink on her cheeks, another bite of chili before she says quietly, "*I* noticed."

I want to ask what else she noticed, if anything she's noticed might be something she wants, but—

Too soon.

I should just be happy I'm here, that she's talking to me without the crutch of a flat tire.

That she's let me touch her.

Speaking of which, I dare to reach forward, to touch her again. And as I swipe my thumb over the corner of her mouth, I have to resist the urge to lean in and flick my tongue along the spot.

"Wh-what?" she asks.

"You had a little chili," I say, bringing my thumb to my mouth, cock twitching at her soft inhalation.

"Oh," she whispers, sinking into shy.

But even as I'm reaching for something to say, something that will help the shy retreat, she pushes her bowl away and picks up a slice of bread.

Something I know she likes because I've heard her wax poetic to the girls about the healing properties of sourdough bread with "the perfect, crunchy, chewy crust" many times over.

I just didn't know that she loved it enough to out-eat me.

It's impressive.

So I'm smiling when she says, "Tell me about Blake."

My smile widens.

"You love him."

"I do." I nod. "He's hilarious and smart and a"—I wink at her—"pain in my ass. But he's *my* pain in the ass and he always has my back." I push away my own empty bowl and snag one of the few remaining pieces of bread. "I trust him to tell me when I'm being a dumbass and know that he'll help me get my head straight."

"I love that for you."

"Me too," I say quietly. "He's all the best parts of me and none of the bad."

Her head tilts to the side again, ponytail swinging. "What are the bad parts?"

"You expect me to give you that ammunition?"

She laughs. "Yes, I do."

Hell, if I *wouldn't* give it to her.

But before I can, she stands up and takes our empty bowls to the sink.

"I can get that," I say, following her and snagging the dishes out of her hands.

"I—"

"You cooked. I'll wash up."

"I dumped things in a crockpot, that's hardly cooking."

"Stubborn." I tug at the end of her ponytail.

"I'm not the one who's being stubborn," she says as I move to the sink.

"Why don't you tell me about *that?*" I nod toward the pile of papers on the corner of the island.

She grabs the rest of the dirty dishes, drops them into the sink, then turns and leans back against the counter as I start washing our bowls. "Papers to grade."

"That's a big stack."

Her mouth twitches.

"What?"

"There's a joke there, is all." She smirks. "Too much time around hockey players."

"Rude."

"Maybe." Her smirk widens. "Or maybe, *rude* will be

asking you what it is the guys give you shit about." She winks. "You did promise to dish after I spilled my guts about my boss."

"You're right," I say as I put the bowls in the dishwasher. "I *did* say that."

She scoops up the leftovers into a container, puts it in the fridge. "Well?"

"Well what?" I ask, being deliberately obtuse.

"*Well*, share all the gory details, my friend."

"Maybe I will." I wipe my hands on a towel. "For the right price."

# ELEVEN

## KY

"PR-PRICE?" I stutter.

He sets the towel aside and moves toward me, all lean, coiled strength and grace personified.

On the ice, he moves like liquid silk.

Off it, he's power and finesse and—

He stops, the toes of our shoes brushing, his body mere inches from mine.

"For a kiss," he murmurs. "I'll tell you what the guys give me shit about."

"I—"

God, what would it be like to kiss this man?

This man who's so beautiful and gentle and kind and who has a streak of mischief in him that calls to the sassy little sister in me. I want to tease back.

I *want* to shock the hell out of him, want to lift up on my tiptoes, press my lips to his, and kiss the hell out of him.

But even as I shift forward, the weight moving to my toes,

my heels lifting ever so slightly off the floor in preparation of closing the distance between our mouths—

Fear slices through me, its talons breaking skin, the grip so sudden that I can't brace for it, so fierce it's almost a physical pain.

Because the last time I kissed a man, he—

I drop back onto my heels, skitter back a step.

Then another.

Because I haven't been this close to a strong, powerful man who I want to kiss, a man who could *hurt* me...

Not since that night.

Since that man *had* hurt me.

I back up further, gasping in pain when the sharp edge of the counter jabs into my hip.

"Kylie. *Kylie!*"

The volume, the sharpness of my name on Colt's tongue tells me that this isn't the first time he's called out to me.

Then he's suddenly in my face, reaching for me.

I flinch back. "Don't!"

I know he won't hurt me, but the past and present are tangled together, the nightmare too close, too ready to take over.

He freezes, hands an inch from my body. They hover there for a second before they drop to his sides.

"Please don't touch me," I say, my words barely audible to my own ears.

"Okay," he murmurs. "Okay, baby. I'm not going to touch you. In fact, I'm...going to go over here." He retreats, putting several feet between us and I hate that the distance loosens my lungs, makes it easy to follow his next words, his gentle order. "Just breathe, yeah?"

"Y-yeah," I manage to push out, but my eyes are filling with tears, my cheeks are burning with embarrassment.

With shame.

Why am I still like this?

"I'm sorry," I whisper when the silence has settled between us for so long I can't stand it.

"What the fuck could you possibly be sorry for?"

"I—" My throat closes up and I sink down to the floor, curling my legs in, resting my forehead on my knees as I admit the miserable truth, "I hate that I'm still like this."

"Human?" he asks softly.

That does something to my heart, something I can't think about right now. "Broken," I whisper.

There's another pause, longer. Heavier.

"Baby," he murmurs.

And even though shame wants me to keep my head down, I find that I can't.

I lean back against the cabinets, every muscle in my body so tight, I know it'll only take the slightest push to send me over the edge.

To shatter.

"I'm broken," I whisper. "I...I don't know how to do this, *haven't* done this since—" The memories flash through my brain like a slideshow of terror, of torment.

Pain and fear.

Struggling to stay conscious afterward.

Damon's face.

The police who responded. The hospital staff.

The charges...being dropped.

But not those against Damon.

Oh no, the district attorney made sure my brother's vigilante justice was prosecuted.

"Kylie," Colt murmurs. "Breathe, baby. Just breathe."

I hadn't even realized my lungs are working desperately, taking in short, staccato breaths, that my head is spinning.

I suck in a breath, hold it until my pulse begins to steady then force myself to slowly release it.

"Want me to go?" he says once I've done that a few times.

"No," I whisper.

Because it's the truth.

Because this night, these couple of hours—hell, even every stolen minute on the side of that dark road with Colt has made me feel alive.

Not like I'm muscling my way through life, determined to not let the world see how fucked up I am.

To not let *Damon* see.

He has enough guilt.

He doesn't need me to add to the weight he carries.

Doesn't need to see me clinging by my fingernails, forcing myself to be the person I *was*.

But tonight, for a little while, I was just...me.

Not a broken girl, not a victim.

Just Kylie.

Except, I can't even kiss the man I want, the man who has been patient and sweet and clearly wants to spend time with me without having a panic attack.

"I'm so tired of this shit," I whisper.

A pause. Then, "What shit?"

I meet his deep brown eyes. "You know," I say softly. "You *know*."

His face, fuck it's so damned gentle that my heart squeezes, my eyes burn. "I'm coming over there."

My lips part, ready to protest...

But I don't want to.

So I just nod and hold my breath, waiting for the panic to rise up again as he slowly comes over.

Only it doesn't because—

"What are you doing?"

And now laughter is bubbling up instead of worry.

Because he's doing the goofiest sort of half shimmy, half butt scooch until he's facing opposite me, his back against the perimeter cabinet, his legs stretched out alongside mine.

Close.

But still giving me an exit.

Giving me laughter and safety and...fuck, now my throat is tight for a whole other reason.

"There," he says, "that's better, yeah?"

"Yeah," I murmur.

"Now, what shit?"

I can't bring myself to answer...but I find I don't have to, not with the knowledge that bleeds into his eyes. "You know," I whisper.

He sighs and shakes his head, gaze sliding from mine, a muscle in his jaw flickering. "I know," he eventually says. "And I wish the fucker wasn't off playing in Europe because I'd deliver a beating far more severe than what your brother gave him."

Maybe I should protest, should take the moral high ground.

But the bastard who raped me took...

Too damned much.

"Sometimes I wish he was dead," I admit. "But then I have a nightmare or"—I dare to meet his eyes again—"there's a man I want to get closer to and the terror takes over and I know that it wouldn't matter if he was dead or in prison, he'd still be *here*." I tap my temple.

The rage in Colt's gaze...it sends my pulse skittering.

But his voice, when it finally comes long moments later, is gentle.

So damned gentle I want to crawl into his lap...and then swat at his chest, reminding him that I'm not fragile.

Except, I kind of am.

No.

Not *kind of.*

I'm fragile. I'm breakable. I'm—

"A survivor," Colt says gently. "You're here. You're alive. You've built a life, friendships. You didn't let it destroy you, starfire."

I inhale. "It doesn't feel that way."

He nudges my foot with his. "But that doesn't change the truth."

"The truth that I've never had an orgasm that I didn't give myself?" I blurt. "That I've never felt pleasure from a man's touch because I was a fucking virgin before he raped me and now I'm too scared to try again?"

He freezes.

Then he bursts to his feet.

It's so sudden I flinch back, my head colliding with the cabinets.

"Fuck," he hisses. He lifts a hand, eyes mournful. "Kylie, I —" A sigh. "Fuck, I'm sorry."

Then he's gone, striding from the kitchen and into the hall, the front door closing with a firm *click* behind him.

Closing my eyes, I drop my forehead back against my knees.

Well, I royally screwed this up, didn't I?

Dinner and conversation and feeling lighter than I had in years to...

Huddled in a ball on the kitchen floor, trying not to cry.

Yup.

Go me.

Sighing, I sit there for a few more moments, waiting until the stinging in my eyes subsides. Then I gather my strength. Prepare to stand.

I have papers to grade, a lunch to make for tomorrow.

An appointment to make to get my tire—

"How can I help?"

Gasping, my head flies up, and I see Colt standing in the doorway.

"Wh-what?"

He comes over to me, slow and steady, crouching in front of my bent knees. "How can I help, starfire?"

I want to ask why he keeps calling me that.

Want to ask why he came back.

Want to ask what he can possibly see in a broken woman.

Instead, what comes out is,

"You can give me something better."

# TWELVE

## COLT

HER MOUTH CLAMPS CLOSED, as though she can't believe she's said that out loud, her cheeks flaring bright red, her eyes skating away.

Give her something better?

I'd give her *anything* she asked for.

So, it's not even a second thought to say, "Okay."

Now her mouth falls open, eyes going wide. "I—uh—"

I cross over to her, extend my hand.

Those eyes go wider. "Uh...I'm...*now?*"

The scandalized look on her face almost has me smiling. "Let's take a walk, starfire."

She exhales. "Oh."

Then she places her hand in mine, allowing me to draw her up, to guide her to the front door I intended to leave through, intended to go and to walk off this rage inside me. Yet I found myself not able to step across the threshold, not with her hurting in the other room. Pausing to snag her coat, I help her into it before I twist the handle and lead us out into the night air.

It's cool and quiet, a thousand stars overhead.

Fucking beautiful, and even though it's something I've seen many times over since I moved to Tahoe, the sight of that dark sky full of glittering diamonds is still one of the most beautiful things I've ever seen.

But it doesn't even begin to compare to the woman who's standing next to me, our hands linked.

*Please don't touch me.*

*I'm broken.*

Yet, she's here.

With me, courage and strength in that slender body that shouldn't have had to shelter so much pain.

*I'm so tired of this shit.*

Carrying the weight of her past for too long.

Alone because she doesn't want the world to know she's still hurting, still coping.

Doesn't want her brother to know—

Because he suffered too.

Fuck, do I understand that.

But tonight I don't want to allow that in—the suffering, the pain, the regrets.

I want to give her something better.

"You still want to know what the guys give me shit about?" I ask as we weave through the parking lot and turn onto the faintly lit trail that leads up into the pines she likes to walk along.

She misses a step then tilts her head to the side, face tipping up so I can see her mouth is curved. "Without the aforementioned payment?"

My mouth quirks. "Consider this one on the house."

"Okay."

"No mercy, huh?" I ask as we start making our way up the slight outcropping.

A sound of pure outrage. "You're the one who offered!"

"Maybe I didn't expect you to take me up on it," I counter, drawing her a little closer when the trail drops off, not wanting her that near to the edge.

"Maybe," she says, her eyes flicking up to mine, something in the depths telling me she knew exactly what I was doing with that maneuver. "Or maybe you're trying to distract me."

"Is it working?"

She laughs then slips her hand from mine as we crest the final hill, moving to sit on a fallen log. "No," she says, patting the spot beside me. "Tell me."

She's laughing.

Smiling.

At me.

No fear, no tears, no panic.

Just the beautiful sky overhead and the beauty that is Kylie.

So, I can no more stop myself from walking over to the log and sitting next to her than I could stop my heart from beating.

Same as I can no more stop myself from telling her what my share of the locker room shit-giving is about.

"No, you didn't!" she gasps.

I nod. "Would I lie to you?"

Her head tilts to the side, gaze locked with mine, eyes suddenly serious. "I hope not," she says quietly. "But I don't know you well enough to say for certain."

That's fair.

More than fair.

It still feels like an actual physical blow though. A blocked shot missing my pads, the puck colliding with exposed flesh.

"Colt," she says quietly.

"In this case, unfortunately, I'm telling the truth."

A pause, then her eyes dance, her reply quiet. "Brutal."

"Some might say it was well-earned."

"I'm not so sure about that." She exhales. "But it *is* hockey."

"Exactly." I wink and she smiles at me before she returns her focus to the vista in front of us. It's dark, only a few lights glimmering in the distance, but it's enough to outline the shadows of the trees, the border of the lake.

I know if we walked all the way to its edge we'd hear the soft lapping of the waves on the shore, if we dipped our fingers inside it would be icy cold.

"Tell me about the papers?"

She ducks her head and I know if it was light, her cheeks would be pink.

"Tell me," I order, turning my body on the log so I'm facing her.

She nibbles at her lip but when she looks up at me, mischief is creeping back into her eyes.

"What?"

"I guess..." She sighs and turns to face me, mirroring my position. "I guess you showed me yours so I should show you mine."

A flicker of heat in my belly, sliding down, wrapping invisible fingers around my dick and stroking.

I ignore it, know there's no room for it, not right now.

Not when I have to give her something good.

"You don't owe me anything," I begin.

"Don't I?"

"Baby—"

She presses a finger to my mouth, halting my words. "I'm a terrible grader. There." She tosses up her hands. "I admitted it, okay? Every year—hell, every quarter, I have the best of intentions. I tell myself I'm going to stay ahead of the papers, give the kids their essays back on time, and it never fails that I find something 'more important' to do and the papers start multiplying."

"They do that?" I ask lightly.

"Like bacteria," she says in a mock-grumble. "Within twenty-four hours they start reproducing—one paper turns into two turns into four turns into sixteen. And then I'm overrun."

My reply is dry. "I didn't know they could do that."

She grins up at me. "Didn't you?"

Fuck, she's beautiful.

"What are these *more important* things?" I ask lightly. "The ones that cause your grading to start reproducing?"

Her grin widens. "Oh you know," she says off-handedly.

"I *don't* know." A beat. "Hence why I asked."

"*Hence?* That's a big word for a big, dumb hockey player," she teases, mimicking my earlier words.

I tug lightly at her ponytail. "Brat."

She giggles. "Just channeling my younger sisterliness."

If there's anything I'm thinking about Kylie, it sure as fuck isn't sisterly.

"Still, considering Damon is your brother, I don't think you're unfamiliar with hockey players using big words."

"Maybe not."

"There's no *maybe* about it."

She laughs. "Crocheting and reality TV and wine."

The conversational left turn has my brows dragging together. "What?"

"The *more important* things."

I get it then and I chuckle. "Well, considering I've seen what you call *crocheting*, I don't think that can reasonably be blamed for the lack of grading."

"Hey!" She glares at me. "Who's being the bratty sibling now?"

I want to kiss that frown off her face.

The urge is so strong, so all-encompassing I almost do exactly that.

But she's not ready.

So, I just stand. "Come on."

The glare gives way to confusion. "What?"

I start down the hill.

"Colt?" she calls. "Where are you going?"

My lips twitch as I glance over my shoulder at her.

"To grade some papers."

# THIRTEEN

## KY

"TELL me that ChatGPT was used without telling me that ChatGPT was used," Colt says on a groan, tossing the essay aside and reclining back on my couch. "How do you deal with this shit?"

I laugh and toss my own paper aside. "I don't," I say, sweeping my hand out at the stack that's barely gone down in size, even though we've been at it for what feels like hours.

(But it is really only thirty minutes).

"Should we give them all As?" he asks, leaning forward and picking up the essay again.

"Even the ChatGPT one?"

His expression is so disgruntled, I can't help but laugh again. "You really don't have to do this, you know that, right?"

He sobers then slowly lifts his free hand.

It's tentative, cautious.

Part of me hates it with an intensity that makes me want to

overturn the coffee table, to launch my wineglass against the wall, painting it red with the chardonnay.

But that would be a waste of perfectly good wine.

And it would ignore the other part of me, the *bigger* part.

The part that's warmed by his actions, soothed by the way he wants to take care of me, healed that he's seen the broken pieces and he's still here...

Grading papers.

He tucks a strand of hair behind my ear. "I *want* to be here."

My lungs seize and even as I'm absorbing the impact of that, of how good it feels, he sits back.

"You know what would make this better?" he asks.

"More wine?" I quip.

Lips twitching, he shakes his head.

"Even *more* wine?"

A chuckle. "No, baby."

My heart feels like a skittish jackrabbit leaping about in my chest. "Then what?" I ask quietly.

He leans close, close enough for that jackrabbit to transform into an elephant.

He has a scar near the corner of his mouth and I want to trace it with my fingers, with my lips...my tongue.

His breath is on my skin, his body is close.

But before I can feel that, before I can get lost in that...or the panic that's sure to cling to its coattails, he snags the remote from the coffee table and points it at the receiver.

"Reality TV."

---

"Baby," I hear from a distance. "Baby, wake up."

I'm warm and comfortable, cuddled against a pillow that smells like spice, a pillow that's warm and...*hard?*

I blink, trying to claw myself out of the depths of sleep.

The next thing I'm aware of are fingers stroking through my hair, gentle and steady, and then that hard, spicy pillow...

Or Colt's thighs, rather.

I'm sprawled out on the couch, my head in his lap—

My eyes fly open on a gasp.

"Easy," he says quietly, glancing down at me, those fingers never stopping their gentle movements. "You fell asleep, baby. But it's getting late, I should head home, let you go up to bed."

"You fell asleep too," I say softly.

He's deliciously sleep-rumpled, a lock of hair having fallen forward to tumble over his forehead, his lids heavy, the stubble on his jaw longer than normal, calling for *my* fingers to stroke.

His mouth kicks up. "Yeah, I did."

Quiet falls between us and it's not strange, not scary.

It's...comfortable.

"You didn't like the show?" I ask softly, knowing I should move, but unable to make myself sit up.

"I'm not the only one who crashed out between dinner parties gone wrong and obscenely large shopping trips."

"Rude," I say. "I had a trying day"—and three glasses of wine, but who was counting?—"that's the only reason *I* fell asleep."

"Touché." He chuckles and I finally make myself sit up.

"Was it that bad?" I tease.

"The show or the grading?"

"Either." My blood is full of champagne, leaving me feeling joyful and effervescent. "Both."

"Terrible," he teases back, holding up a hand with pen and pencil stains along the inside. "And I've been marked."

"Your fault for being a lefty," I counter.

"Now that's a rude thing to say to the person who helped you get through that stack." A nod at the now-graded pile of papers. "I expected gratitude and instead I'm getting sass."

Amusement in my belly. "I think you like the sass."

"I think"—he tucks that unruly strand of hair behind my ear again—"I like anything and everything about you, Kylie Connors."

That amusement morphs, turning into pleased surprise, into tentative hope, into a yearning to grasp tightly to this moment that's not clouded with the past.

"Colt," I whisper, shifting an inch closer.

Warmth in his eyes.

No. *Heat* in those gorgeous brown eyes of his. They darken, turning the color of melted chocolate, tempting me to dip a finger in, to bring it to my mouth, to...

*Taste.*

God, I want to taste.

And that's...

Well, it's not scary.

Holy heck, it's *not* scary.

I lean an inch closer, testing myself, trying to find the edge of my control, where that panic begins to crawl up and take over, to suck the pleasure out of this moment.

But the inch doesn't do that.

So, I take another.

Then another.

Then suddenly freeze when I realize exactly how close I am to him, our bodies almost touching, our mouths a bare few centimeters apart.

He's still, the only movement that of his lungs, his breaths coming fast.

So are mine.

"I—"

But I can't find the right words, can't give voice to the need that's burning inside me.

"Take it," he murmurs.

My pulse hitches. "Wh-what?"

"What you want."

"I—"

He spreads his hands on his thighs, fingers clenching at the material of his jeans. "I won't move, won't touch. You can just..." He licks his lips, eyes sliding to the side then coming back to mine, hot and tempting. "You can just take what you want and I'll stay exactly like this."

My heart hiccups, starts beating rapidly, trying to escape the cage of my lungs.

"What about what *you* want?"

His fingers flex, digging into the hard muscles of his legs.

His jaw clenches, a muscle flickering along the defined edge.

But it's his eyes that steal my breath.

Because they burn into mine as he says,

"What I want more than my next heartbeat is too feel your lips on mine."

# FOURTEEN

## COLT

I HOLD MY BREATH, thinking I've blown it.

That she'll pull back.

My fingers are clenched so tightly into my thighs they're cramping.

But I still don't move.

Not as the moment stretches.

Not as her body shifts away from mine ever so slightly and disappointment slices through my abdomen.

Fuck.

She's going to—

In a sudden rush of movement, she closes the distance between our bodies.

One second, I'm fighting that crippling disappointment and the next, I'm stunned stupid by the feel of her body against mine.

Soft hands on my shoulders, lush tits pressed to my side... lips that taste like heaven taking mine.

It's the sweetest kiss of my life—gentle and easy, her mouth sipping at mine.

It takes everything in me to keep my hands on my legs, to not put them on her body, to not dive them into her hair, deepening the kiss. Hell, it takes everything in me to follow her lead and not part my lips, to not plunge my tongue into her mouth and taste her like I'm desperate to.

But I let her lead.

Even as one of her hands slides up my neck and into my hair, fisting the strands tightly, sending little sensual bites of pain along my nape.

It doesn't hurt, not really.

But it does further erode my control.

"More," I rasp when she pulls back.

More hands on my body. More lips against mine. Just... *more*.

Her mouth curves and she shifts closer, kissing me again. Only this time it's *more*. More lips. More tongue. More of her gorgeous body pressed to mine.

She strokes her tongue against the seam of my mouth and I part my lips, allowing her inside.

Her moan is soft, but it's the best thing I've ever heard, and the way she brushes her breasts against my arm, tightens her hand in my hair...

More of my control eroded.

More need coiling in my stomach.

More cramping in my fingers.

"You taste good," she whispers.

"Like fucking ambrosia," I rasp, digging my fingers into my jeans, knowing I'm probably giving myself bruises but not able to summon one flying fuck about it. "More?" I ask.

Or maybe beg.

Either way, there's a flicker of mischief, of sultry feminine confidence in those gorgeous blue eyes.

And then I get her mouth back on mine, her body pressing closer, those gentle strokes of her tongue, the firm grip of my hair, the softness of her body against the hardness of mine.

I've never had a more addictive drug.

But I know when she breaks away to suck in another breath and then her grip tightens and she leans in again that she's had enough.

She's as under the influence of desire as I am.

And it would only take one slight nudge to send her in the wrong direction, to have that panic sweeping up and taking over.

To steal this from her too.

So, I finally release my legs, the blood burning through my flesh as I slowly catch her shoulder, staying her before her mouth can find mine again.

"Enough, baby."

Her eyes are dilated, her lips are swollen, and she blinks dazedly. "Wh-what?"

"That's enough for tonight, baby."

"I—what?"

Smiling, I slide my hand down along her arm until I can lace my fingers through hers and draw her up to her feet. "Walk me out, starfire?"

A blink.

Another.

Then she shakes her head as though to clear it. "You're going?"

"You need to go to bed," I remind her. "And I need to pack for the road trip."

"R-right," she whispers.

But her eyes skate away...and there's something in them that I don't like.

"What is it?" I ask when she tries pull her hand from mine. I hold on, but only for a second then reluctantly allow her fingers to slip free.

"Nothing," she says softly. "Let's get your coat and shoes—"

"Kylie."

She starts for the door and I hurry to catch her, taking my jacket that she holds out. But I don't step into the boots she toes in my direction. "What is it?"

A shake of her head. "Like I said, nothing."

"Not *nothing*." I step closer, crouch a little to see her eyes. "Tell me."

She's quiet for so long, I think she's not going to, that she'll close down and tell me to go—and I would.

Because I don't think I could deny this woman anything.

"Please," I murmur.

More quiet, but her gaze comes back to mine, lingers, her cheeks going pink.

"I..." Her mouth opens, closes, then her eyes go over my shoulder. "Well, I..." She nibbles at her bottom lip. "You know I'm not...all that..."

I nod encouragingly, wait patiently (or at least, patiently on the outside) as she finds the right words.

"I'm not all that experienced," she whispers. "And I haven't..." Her throat works. "Obviously, I haven't done that for a long time. I..."

I wait, wishing I could draw her close, could taste her again, could—

"Well, was that...okay?"

On a list of questions I was expecting her to ask, that wouldn't even have been in the top thousand.

In fact, it takes me by so much surprise, I laugh.

Which isn't the right move in this situation—not even in the top thousand.

She slides back a step, cheeks going pinker.

"Kylie," I murmur, catching her fingers, keeping her in place. "Baby."

"It's okay," she says, not looking at me. "I know I'm not any good at—"

I press her hand to my pelvis, to where my dick is currently trying to poke its way out of my jeans. "If you were any better at it, baby, I'd be taking this somewhere you're not ready to go."

Her fingers flex, curving around the hard length of my erection, and I bite back my groan.

"Oh," she whispers.

"Yeah." I peel her palm free. "*Oh.*"

Her smile...fuck, it's adorable.

And tempting.

I want to taste it.

I want to do a fuck of a lot more than kiss her again.

So, I step back.

Shove my feet into my boots and do them up.

Tug on my jacket.

It's only when I've unlocked and opened the door that I dare touch her again.

I brush the backs of my knuckles along her cheek.

"Only good dreams tonight, starfire."

# FIFTEEN

## KY

ONLY GOOD DREAMS TONIGHT, *starfire*.

I bite the inside of my cheek, hiding my smile.

Mostly because I need to focus.

I've thought of those words far too many times over the last few days.

And they never fail to make me feel...

Warm.

Okay, *hot* really.

Remembering the taste of Colt's mouth, the feel of his body against mine.

The rasp of his voice.

How he'd held himself so carefully still and let me take the lead.

And the need that had coiled itself so tautly in my belly when he brought my hand to his—

Laughter ricochets through my classroom and I jerk myself sharply into focus.

It's a half day before a long holiday weekend and the kids are nuts.

They don't want to be here and...frankly, neither do I.

Because the team arrived back in town this morning.

More laughter, followed by a strong "Shh!"

Now I smother a grin.

Most of us don't want to be here...with the exception of Adrian.

Today is his first day back and he's his typical bright, lovely self. I just want to hug him close and tell him how glad I am that he's here.

But I already did that once.

He's an eleven-year-old boy. He barely tolerated the first round of my fussing.

He certainly won't accept another.

So, I'd better get my shit together.

"Who loves fat cats?" I call over the laughter.

"We love fat cats!" the class calls back.

There's snickering and more laughter, but it's controlled now, their focus coming to me. Some teachers say *I'm waiting.* Some flick off the lights. Some clap their hands.

I...well, I talk about fat cats.

And it works every time.

I get the smiles, the laughter, the eye rolls.

But I also get their attention.

"All right," I say. "It's short periods today so let's get what we need to get done, yeah?"

Groans all around.

"Because if we do, I have a Kahoot for you and"—I walk over to my desk, pull open the top drawer—"the top three scores will win..." With a flourish I pull out the bag of candy I picked up from the discount aisle at the grocery store. "Their choice of deliciousness."

Competitiveness, their stomachs, and a dash of learning.

It's all I can hope to accomplish on a minimum day.

I get through my slides, foster a short discussion, and seed in the next bit of prep for their upcoming end of semester project.

*Then* it's time for fun.

They have their Chromebooks open and are battling it out over historical empires when I hear a knock at the door.

It's policy to keep it locked—because this is America and school intruders are an unfortunate reality—but there's a narrow window that means I can see who's on the other side... and when I make eye contact with the person who's knocked my pulse skips a beat...or maybe a dozen of them.

The class groans—my history quiz has a few tricky questions, the better to keep their focus, muahaha—and I snap to attention, hurrying to the door and pulling it open a couple of inches.

"Colt?" I hiss through the crack. "What are you doing here?"

The class groans again and Colt smiles. "Sounds like they're having fun in there."

It did.

But the online game will only last for so long.

"I—" I clench the edge of the door.

"Ms. Connor?"

I jerk and spin to see Adrian. He's rail thin and wearing a mask, but he's here, and determined. "Look! I got first place."

I grin.

Because of course he did.

"Nice, Adrian." I hold up my fist for him to bump. "You get first choice from the candy bag."

"I'm second," Lara says, pointing her screen in my direction.

I nod. "You know the drill."

She jumps up and I glance toward the whiteboard at the front of the classroom where the winners are displayed. "Who's..." I pause, having taught for long enough to know exactly what the seventh grade mind was thinking when he or she named themself.

Gabe H. Coud

Douchebag backwards.

Cute.

But the smirk on Vince's face isn't.

"Vince, pick your candy," I finish. "But," I add as he clambers to his feet and hustles toward my desk, "you and I will be having a chat at the end of class."

His smirk fades and his eyes come to mine, as if gauging my seriousness.

I just lift my eyebrows.

His shoulders hunch, but he nods.

"Good catch," I hear murmured in my ear and jump slightly, having forgotten that Colt was there.

*How*, I don't know.

Not when every nerve in my body is alive, sparking with sensation.

"You too," I say softly.

"Me too what?"

"You and I need to have a chat at the end of class."

His mouth quirks. "Whatever you say, Teach."

Warmth in my belly, dipping between my legs. But I just pull the door wider so he can slip inside then lift my chin and point at the row of cabinets near the back of the room. "Wait there."

A wink that has my heart pounding against my ribs.

"Like I said"—he lightly brushes the backs of his knuckles over my cheek—"whatever you say, baby."

That light touch burns through me and it's with shaky knees that I walk up to the front of the class, tucking the treats away and then giving the kids the happy news that their only homework over the long weekend is going to be to go outside and touch grass...then to submit a picture as proof to the online portal.

"Ms. Connors?"

"Yeah?" I say as I finish writing the assignment on the white board ("Touch Grass. Submit Picture.").

"Is he your *boooyfriend?*"

"No—"

"Yes," Colt says at the same time.

My stomach convulses and I open my mouth but things quickly spiral out of my control.

"What's your name?"

"Why are you here?"

"You're really tall?"

"Aren't you the guy who plays for the Sierra?"

"Hockey's boring!"

"Ms. C, are you in *luuuuv?*"

"Ew, boys are gross!"

"Why's he here?"

"Can we pack up? The bell's in five minutes."

"I—" A grunt. "Can't open this."

"My name is Colt," he says. "I do play for the Sierra and boys *can* be gross, but they usually grow out of that." He winks at me again and it's all I can do to keep from swooning. "And we'll have to agree to disagree on the hockey is boring front." His mouth kicks up. "I kind of like it."

The room falls quiet, and I'm certainly not about to be the one to snap out of my stupor enough to break the silence.

Colt is the only one who's nonplussed.

He moves over to Adrian and tears open the packet of candy. "Wash your hands before you eat it," he says softly.

"Can I have your autograph?" Simon asks.

A shrug. "Sure, if you somehow think that it's worth something."

I frown—because why wouldn't it be worth something?

But the kids keep talking before I can truly process his statement.

"My dad said that the goal you had in the shootout was the best thing he's ever seen." A grin. "Well, he said it was the best *something* thing he's ever seen, but Ms. C gets mad when I use those words in school."

"Probably a good idea not to use them then," Colt says dryly, flicking his gaze toward me, eyes sparkling with humor. "Not a good idea to make Ms. C mad."

"You're telling me," another of the boys says. "Last time she got mad, we had to do pushups."

"Yeah?" Another amused look in my direction. "How many did you do?"

"Twenty-two."

"Impressive."

"I did twenty-five."

"Killing it, dude."

"Well, I only did ten."

"That's still good."

"I did sixteen!"

"Awesome, kiddo."

"I didn't do anything," Adrian says quietly. "I *can't* do anything."

And the room goes still.

*Damn.*

I open my mouth, mind flicking through responses, trying to find the right one.

But my class beats me to it.

"But you're like a real-life superhero," Sylvia says. "You've had like a billion surgeries and you're back in school."

My eyes burn.

Because these kids can be brutally honest—hell, they can just be brutal. But they can also be wonderful.

Like right now.

"Totally," Simon says. "My mom said you've survived death, like, a dozen times. That's killer."

I wince.

But I don't interject because Adrian doesn't look upset.

In fact, he sits a little straighter, his chin coming up. "*My* mom says that all of this has made me stronger."

"She's right," Colt says quietly.

"Really?" he asks, face filled with hope.

"Really," he says.

"I agree," I interrupt. Because the kids are being awesome, but they're still seventh graders and their ability to tamp down the snark is limited. Better to quit while we're ahead. "And I think it's time for everyone to pack up so you're not late for your next period," I say before anyone can ruin the niceness of the moment. "Vince, you're with me."

Colt's mouth twitches, but the bell goes right then and any response is lost in the chaos of the kids packing up and hurrying out the door and the short, quiet warning I give my class clown.

But I don't miss that Colt signs the slip of paper Simon holds up.

And I don't miss him crouching beside Adrian's desk, saying something that has my young charge's face lighting up.

"Bye, Ms. C!" someone calls.

I wave, even as my heart threatens to beat out of my chest.

"Bye, Ms. C's boyfriend!" someone else calls.

A soft, masculine chuckle.

One I hear because Colt has straightened and walked over to me.

"Hi," he murmurs.

"Hi," I murmur back.

"Your kids are great," he says as they file out the door, leaving the room quiet...for about two more minutes.

Then my next period will roll in.

"Yeah, they are." I lean back against my desk. "Why are you here?"

He shifts closer, reaching out and taking my hand. "I needed to see you."

My lips part on a shaky exhale. "Colt," I murmur.

"Come have dinner with me tonight."

"I—"

"Just dinner."

"I—"

"Don't say no."

"I—"

"Please."

"*Colt.*"

His mouth snaps closed, teeth clicking together.

I squeeze his hand then pull mine free as my next period starts rolling in.

"I was just going to ask what time?"

# SIXTEEN

## COLT

THE DOORBELL RINGS as I'm sliding the pan into the oven.

It's nothing special, just some roasted potatoes and chicken breasts seasoned with breadcrumbs, rosemary, and a dash of hot honey.

The dessert that's percolating in the fridge is killer, though.

Lemon parfaits with freshly whipped cream and strawberries that cost almost ten bucks for a tiny carton.

But they're ripe and fresh and Kylie's favorite.

*One* of her favorites, anyway.

Because her favorite food is dessert.

Yup. Just *dessert*.

Mouth twitching, I close the oven, snag a towel to wipe my hands and hurry to the front door, pulling it open and—

My lungs freeze.

She is so fucking beautiful.

She's changed since I saw her at school, trading her slacks

and fitted tee and cardigan for a long skirt and a sweater that caresses the curves I'm desperate to touch, to stroke, to lick and kiss and bite.

But it's the pumps that are currently on her feet that have my dick going hard.

High and sleek, made of a dark brown material and with a slender, spiked heel I want digging into my back.

"Colt?" she whispers.

And I realize I've been staring at her, thinking about those heels, that skirt rucked up around her waist.

And *not* about stepping back and letting her into my house.

A house she was uncomfortable in the last time she was over.

A house I want her spending a fuck-ton more time in.

Something that won't happen if I just stand here like an idiot, staring at her.

"Sorry, Teach," I say lightly as I move so she can come in. "I like the shoes," I can't help but add.

She pauses, glances over her shoulder, eyes filled with a feminine confidence that has my already hard dick going harder. "Thanks."

And then she just *click-clicks* her way down the hall, hips swaying in a way I know isn't intentional...but is still inflammatory.

At least for my dick.

Shaking myself, I close and lock the door.

"Something smells delicious," she says as I join her in the kitchen.

"Nothing fancy."

"Nothing fancy like your lasagna with the homemade noodles?" she asks. "Or nothing fancy like us normal people would make on a weeknight?" She holds out a bottle of wine I didn't even realize she'd carried in, I was so distracted by those heels.

By the way the fabric of that ankle-length skirt cups her curves.

How the sweater clinging to her breasts looks soft and pettable...

And how I want to pet every inch of her.

My dick goes harder, straining against my zipper.

"I like how you look at me," she murmurs.

"It doesn't scare you?"

She shakes her head. "No." Teeth pressing into her bottom lip. "It makes me *want*."

*Fuck.*

"Don't say that, Teach."

"Why?" she whispers. "I keep thinking about the kiss on the couch, keep thinking about how I missed you when you were gone, keep thinking about how good you were with the kids today."

"They're good kids," I manage to push out.

"Yes, they are."

"And they clearly like and respect you."

A slender shoulder shrugs. "I bribe them with candy."

I chuckle. "Nice try, but I didn't miss the adoring looks."

Her cheeks go slightly pink, but she nods to the bottle. "Will that go with whatever it is that you've cooked up?"

"Do you like it?"

"It's my favorite."

"Then it goes with my food."

"Colt," she begins.

I shake my head and move to the cabinets, pulling down two glasses, then digging through a drawer to retrieve the wine opener.

I pour the chardonnay, pass her a glass. "It's not that serious." I pick up my own glass. "I promise. Now, tell me how the rest of your day went."

When she doesn't immediately speak, I lean back on the counter and prompt. "Adrian seemed like he was having a good first day back. Did you hear anything from his other—"

*Clink.*

It sounds dangerous—like the glass is breaking—but even as I turn to ask Kylie if she's okay, she's launching herself into my arms, her mouth seeking mine.

"Baby," I begin, pulling back, not nearly in enough control to do this right now.

To feel her body against mine and not take.

To have her kissing me, her tongue in my mouth, her hands on me...no, I need to sip her up in slow, controlled draws, be patient as I give her something good—and *only* something good.

I can't have her looking at me with fear and panic in her eyes again.

I fucking *can't.*

She freezes when I draw away, hands clenched on my thighs again, fingers desperate to touch, to stroke, to tease. "You don't—" Bright red cheeks. "I thought you coming to school..." She drops back onto her heels. "I thought dinner..." A step back. "You don't want to?"

I snag her wrist, staying her. "Do I need to show you how much I want you again?"

A shudder, her body swaying toward mine. "Colt," she whispers.

"No?" I ask lightly.

"I don't want to think about it." Her throat works. "About *him.*"

Slowly, I draw her back against me. "I don't want you to think about it either. About him." I slide my hand along her spine, soaking in the feel of her. "But we need to move slowly, need to be patient."

"I just want to get it over with."

My mouth quirks. "Are you saying my kissing skills are that bad?" I tease.

"I—" She breaks off on a sigh and closes her eyes, wincing. "I'm sorry," she says, "I didn't mean it to sound like that. It's just...the other night was so good and you're so wonderful and... you came to school today."

"Did you forget about the tires?" I joke.

"No," she whispers, settling her hand on my chest. "I didn't."

Tenderness blooms in my belly and I bury my face in her hair, inhaling the soft floral scent, feeling the silky strands cling to my beard. "Baby."

She shudders, hand sliding to my stomach and pushing back, those blue eyes unfathomable...at least until she asks, "Kiss me?"

"Are you ready for that?"

Her face goes soft. "I'm ready to try."

I wait for a long moment, giving her time to change her mind, then lean in and brush my lips over hers, once, twice, three times.

A long, slow exhale, her body relaxing against mine.

I brush again, a little harder this time, and when she only sighs again, I deepen the touch of my mouth against hers, dipping my tongue in to tangle with hers.

She moans softly and I slide my hand up her back, drawing her more firmly against me—

And there.

Stiffness between her shoulder blades.

The slightest tremble of her fingers on my stomach.

I pull back, drop my hand.

Her eyes are closed and she sighs, shaking her head. "I'm sorry."

"There's nothing to be sorry about."

"I can't even—"

"*Nothing* to be sorry about."

Another shake. "I should—"

I press my finger to her lips, trying to find the words to make my words clear.

But they don't come.

Because I...*sniff*.

Then groan, hurrying to the oven and pulling open the door.

Black smoke billows out.

"Nothing to be sorry about except for distracting me so much that dinner's toast," I say, slamming it closed and turning off the heat.

When I spin around her expression is chagrined...

And still fucking beautiful.

Especially when she holds up her glass and says,

"At least we have wine?"

# SEVENTEEN

## KY

I EXPECT him to be pissed about dinner.

I would have been—or if not pissed, at least annoyed after spending the time prepping, not to mention the money on the food.

Or maybe it's that I expect him to be upset about my behavior.

Acting like a lunatic—throwing myself at him one moment, panicking on the kitchen floor the next.

Except...I hadn't.

Tonight, I hadn't panicked.

But he knew I was riding that edge, didn't he?

I hadn't missed that was precisely when he pulled back.

Which just makes me like him all that much more.

Same as his smile at my *At least we have wine?*

Now he moves toward me and cups my cheek. "How are you at chopping carrots?"

"I'm better at peeling potatoes," I say, not quite sure where the sass is coming from.

Except...that it's me.

The me I am with my friends. The me I am with Damon.

The me I used to be with men before—

No.

I don't want to think about that, about him. I want to enjoy tonight, enjoy feeling like myself, enjoy...

Just *enjoy*.

"Well," he says, "all the potatoes are currently ash in the oven so you've got your choice of onions, peppers, or carrots."

A flicker of guilt. "Do you want me to order something in? Since I ruined dinner?"

His finger slides down my throat, along my collarbone, and I shiver.

"I think we were both responsible for making charcoal, and I have plenty of food—" His voice rises, drowning out my protests. "So, carrots, onions, or peppers?" He leans in, brushes his lips over my jaw. "Or sitting there looking beautiful while I do the chopping?"

I shiver, give in to the need clawing at me to run my fingers through his beard. "You giving up shaving?"

A lazy shrug. "Didn't have the energy to bother." He searches my face. "You don't like it?"

I think about the slightly rough hairs brushing over my skin...my throat, my breasts, my belly...*lower*...and I shiver.

His mouth tips up. "You like it."

"Arrogant man."

"*Happy* man that I've finally got the beautiful woman who's kept me on tenterhooks for the better part of two years finally flirting with me." He drops his hands to the counter, one on either side of my body. Caging me in.

But I'm not scared.

"This is flirting?" I tease. "Telling me to get in the kitchen?"

"You're already *in* the kitchen." Another brush of his lips over my cheek, my jaw, dragging their way over to my ear. "Now you just need to start cooking."

My hand has somehow made its way into his hair, is clinging tightly to the silky strands, so it takes me a moment to process the words. Then I do, gasping in outrage. "Seriously?" I snap, tugging now, but not hard. Only so I can see his face, can see what I know is going to be in the deep brown eyes.

And yup.

Humor.

Teasing.

Mischief.

And below all of those...*need.*

It sends my pulse skittering through my veins.

Because I have that same need, that same yearning. From the moment I first saw him in the hallways at the Sierra's arena, I was drawn to him.

And now I'm here.

Now I'm learning him.

Now he's smiling and teasing.

Now we've touched, kissed...

"You do the carrots," I say. "I'll do the onions and peppers."

"Anything for you, Teach."

My lungs inflate in a rush.

Because I think he means exactly that.

---

"More?" I ask in disbelief.

"There's no such thing as too much garlic."

"Except when it's so intense that it gives me garlic breath," I protest.

No one wants to kiss a gross, garlicky mouth.

He shoves another clove into the garlic press and squeezes, dropping the extruded contents into the pot of soup he's somehow whipped up.

Lasagna soup because he didn't have enough noodles to make a full pan, but he had the rest of the ingredients.

"Two garlic breaths make a right."

I just shake my head, but I'm smiling and—

Then I'm being kissed—a short, blazing press of his mouth that sets my heart pumping.

"Wh-what are you doing?" I ask as he pulls back, grinning.

"Getting my fill of you before garlic breath."

Startled, I laugh, and he opens his mouth, no doubt to tease me again when his phone rings. He tugs it out of his pocket, silences it. "My brother," he explains.

"Answer it," I say. "I'll keep adding garlic." A beat. "To fend off the vampires and all."

He grins, brushes his mouth over mine, and swipes, lifting his phone to his ear. "Blake," he says, hand settling on my back, fingers brushing lightly over the curve of my hip.

I haven't missed what he's doing with the soft touches, the gentle presses of his mouth.

Getting me used to him being close—to touches from a man that aren't scary, that don't bring pain, that won't drag me back into a nightmare.

Just me and him...

And the fire he's building inside me, one ember at a time.

I exhale, relax into him, am rewarded with his warm body and his spicy scent and the rumble of his voice as he talks to his brother.

"Noodles," he murmurs and it takes a minute for me to realize he's talking to me.

"What?"

"You can add the noodles now," he says, reaching past me and snagging the bowl.

I take it from him, dumping the contents into the pot and stirring.

"Yes"—Colt sighs—"that's a girl."

Amusement has me glancing up at him. He's shaking his head, but his mouth is curved and when his eyes meet mine, they're filled with humor.

"No," I hear. "You don't need to talk to her."

Curiosity blossoms in my belly. "I'd love to talk to him."

An aggrieved look as his chin drops forward, his brows lifting in a silent, *"Really?"*

I smile beatifically. "Really," I murmur.

The phone starts chiming as Blake transitions the call from audio to video. Colt swipes again, points the screen in my direction, and then I'm seeing a face that's much like Colt's, except younger and thinner.

"She's too hot for you, bro."

I suck in a surprised breath.

"Thanks for being cool," Colt grumbles. "Blake, this is Kylie. Kylie, this is Blake."

"Hi, Blake," I say, leaning into his brother a little more heavily, something settling in me when Colt's fingers continue to make small patterns on my hip.

"*Way* too hot for you," Blake says.

"Just because we're related doesn't mean I won't end you," Colt threatens almost cheerfully.

Blake grins. "You could try."

"I would succeed."

"Not hard when all you have to do is unplug a cord and my lungs would quit working."

I jerk, mouth falling open.

"He's joking," Colt tells me, those fingers on my hip becoming soothing.

"Only partially," Blake says, touching the strip of plastic running under his nose. "I need this and a couple other machines, so it would require more than one unplug."

Colt groans, dropping his forehead to my shoulder, the sensation a shock...though not a bad one.

I kind of like it—this big hockey player wrapped around me, leaning on me, even if it's only just a tiny bit.

"Why do I have the feeling that the reason you're so good with my kids is because of this hooligan?" I tease, giving in to the urge to stroke my fingers through the softness of his hair.

"You have kids?" Blake asks.

"She's a middle school teacher," Colt says, the words hot and warm, sinking in through the material of my sweater.

"Yeah? What subject?"

"History," I supply.

"Wicked cool. I love history."

"Go," Colt murmurs, nudging me toward the table. "I'll finish this up."

"But he's your brother. I don't want—"

"Eh, I talk to him all the time," Blake says silkily. "Today, I want to talk to you."

I find myself unable to resist his charm. "Will you give me all the embarrassing stories?"

Colt groans, reaching for the phone. "Maybe I should—"

"Soup," I say, dancing out of reach, knowing my smile is wide.

"Why do I think letting you two talk is a mistake?" he asks.

"Probably because it is?" Blake quips.

I laugh—because I'd been thinking the same thing. Grinning at Colt's brother, I say,

"Oh, I think we're going to get along great."

# EIGHTEEN

## COLT

LAUGHTER DRIFTS down the hall and into the room, sliding over my skin like the softest silk.

Making me go hard...something that doesn't feel great since I'm wearing a cup.

But I ignore it as I get to my feet, breezing by Lake, ignoring the storm cloud that's Storm (kid's going to earn that as his permanent nickname if he doesn't get his shit together), and slipping out into the hallway.

She's there.

My palms itch to touch. My dick twitches and I wince, adjusting it before I move down the hall to her.

She's talking to Damon, who breaks off and lifts a brow at me. "Colt?" he asks when I don't go away.

"I can wait."

His eyes slant toward Kylie. "Go on. I'll catch up to you—"

"Oh, not for you," I say.

His brows fly up.

"I can wait until Kylie's done."

Now they nearly reach his hairline. "You can *wait?*" A beat. "Until Kylie's done?" His tone has murder laced into it, no doubt about that.

"Damon," she begins, setting a hand on her brother's arm. "Don't."

A flickering muscle in his jaw, raging blue eyes—so much like his sister's—locked onto mine. "Don't what?"

"You know what," she says quietly. *Pointedly.* "I'll catch up with you in a bit. *Damon.*"

He finally looks at her and the moment stretches in long, taut silence.

Then he sighs and strides off, anger in each and every line of his body.

Fuck.

Well, that's going to be a problem.

"What are you doing?" she hisses, moving over to me, her hand landing on my chest. The contact sears into me, reminding me of last night, of the touches and kisses I'd snuck over dinner, of her body close to mine when I walked her to her car and kissed her goodnight.

"Did you think I was going to hide us? Hide what we're building?"

She pokes at my pec. "No, but we've had dinner a couple of times, Colt. We've kissed and spent some nights together on the side of the road—"

"Don't."

"Don't what?" she snaps. "Tell the truth? First, you tell my kids that you're my boyfriend—something I should have confronted you about last night, but you distracted me with all your...wonderfulness."

Her scowl is fucking adorable.

But I don't think me kissing it off her lips would go over all that well.

"Maybe it wasn't true then." I tuck the strand of hair behind her ear, the one that always seems to get in her eyes. "But it sure as shit is true now."

Her mouth opens. Closes. "You're kidding me."

"No. It took two years for you to talk to me, to touch me, there's no way I'm going backwards now."

"Well we're not going into warp speed *now*."

"Why not?"

Her eyes bug out of her head. "Why not? Why *not*?" She tosses her hands up and I can't help it.

I smile.

She sees it.

"Oh, my God. You're playing me."

I'm not.

I want nothing more than to have her in my life permanently, as *mine*, not someone else's. Just *mine*.

But I also like the fire in her eyes right now, the way she swats at me.

So, I can wait for her to come around, to accept that she belongs to me.

I can be sneaky and patient.

"Damon isn't happy."

"Like I said"—I touch her cheek—"I won't hide what we're building."

She studies me for a long moment.

Then sighs and shakes her head. "Fine. But no more boyfriend talk."

No fucking way am I agreeing to that.

"I'm serious! Damon could trade you or bench you or—"

"He won't." I brush my knuckles over her cheek, along her throat. "Not only is he too good of a GM to allow that to happen, he wants to see you happy, Teach. As long as I'm doing that, I'm safe." I grin. "Plus, Coach would never agree to it."

She exhales and it's sharp and annoyed and...

Then her eyes go soft.

"Incorrigible."

"You like it."

"No more boyfriend talk."

"Have lunch with me when I get back from the road trip." We're leaving tonight after the game and will be gone almost a week.

Her head tilts to the side, ponytail swinging. "I'll have projects to grade."

"I'll help."

"And steal kisses along the way," she accuses.

I shrug. "Maybe."

"See?" She shakes her head. "Incorrigible."

I lean close, my lips very near her ear. "And see?" I flick out my tongue to taste her, unable to stifle the bolt of arrogant pride that slides through me when she jumps, her hands settling on my shoulders, nails biting into my flesh. Drawing me closer instead of pushing me away. "You like it."

She shudders. "*Colt.*"

"I have it on good authority that you may be able to turn lunch into dinner too."

Her nails dig in harder.

My dick protests the confines of the cup and there's nothing more than I want to do right now than drag her to the nearest dark corner and show her exactly how much I like the feel of her nails on me.

But...slow and patient.

And *sneaky.*

I kiss the delicate, adorable earlobe of hers then straighten. "So, Teach...lunch when I get home?"

A long pause, her eyes going from unfocused to sharp. They hold mine. *Search* mine. Then she nods. "Fine."

"So gracious," I tease.

She sighs, shakes her head as she shoves me in the direction of the locker room. "Get dressed. It's almost time for puck drop."

"Will you be watching?"

"Will you..." Her eyes flick down. "...make it worth my while?"

I wince, try to adjust myself unobtrusively.

But that's nearly impossible.

Especially when her smile grows and she lifts on tiptoe, lips at my ear. "If you do...you might even be able to talk me into breakfast."

Red hazes the edges of my vision.

My dick threatens to break in half.

And then she flicks *her* tongue out to taste *my* earlobe.

My hands drop onto her waist, drawing her against me before I realize what I'm doing, before I can measure her body language, her expression, her eyes for any sign of fear.

But even as I try to force my hands to open, to let her go, she drags her lips along my jaw, brushes her mouth over mine.

"Honey?" she murmurs.

"Y-yeah?" I manage to rasp out.

"Make it good enough and maybe we'll revisit that boyfriend talk."

Then she's slipping out of my arms and I'm watching her saunter down the hallway...

Having the distinct notion that I've been out-sneaked.

# NINETEEN

## KY

"DON'T LOOK at me like that," I mutter, my requisite bucket of buttery popcorn in my hands. "Or I'll be forced to bring up parenthood again."

He pales as he drops down beside me, scowl deepening.

Then he sighs.

"We talked about it."

"Who talked about what?"

A fluttering wave of both palms and fingers, a la jazz hands. "Parenthood," he grits out. "She's scared too." A glance in my direction as I open my mouth, determined to make him understand that he and Joey will be amazing parents.

But then he keeps talking...and his words successfully shut me up.

"We're going to time it so the baby's born in the off-season."

I blink.

Then again.

Then I'm setting my popcorn to the side and lurching to my feet.

He hops to his. "Ky—"

I hug him tightly. "I *cannot* wait to be an auntie. I'm going to spoil the heck out of your kids."

His arms come around me. "I just got used to the idea of *one* kid, now you're throwing kids, plural, at me?"

"You can't just have one," I murmur, even as I'm wondering if I'll ever get there myself when I can't even—

*No.*

Enough.

I'm not shadowing this happy moment with bullshit from the past.

Not when Colt and I—

As though he's plucked the direction of my thoughts out of my mind, he pulls back, hands going to the tops of my arms.

"Kylie," he begins.

"Don't," I murmur. "I..." I exhale. "It's new and he makes me happy and I already have enough shitty thoughts circling around in this brain of mine."

His focus stays on me for a long, long moment.

Then he slides one hand up my arm, along my neck, and cups my jaw. "Okay."

I relax.

"But if he hurts you..."

"Is this where the obligatory *I'll kill him if he hurts you* speech comes in?"

"Don't," he echoes back to me. "I almost lost you once, kid, and you're the only family I have left."

I lean into his touch. "That's not true." A beat. "Not anymore."

A sigh that speaks of a thousand things—our deadbeat dad,

losing our mom, his career going up in smoke, me getting hurt...
and the family we've both become part of since coming here.

"No," he agrees, pulling me into a tight hug. "Not anymore."

Then he nudges me back to my chair, sits down beside me.

I stare at the ice below, aware of the players skating around the rink, but not really processing anything they're doing.

Because of that sigh.

Because of the hope in my brother's hug.

Because of the way he nudges his foot against mine and grins when I look up at him.

"You're the teacher and yet you're talking about spoiling my kids. Aren't you supposed to be the one to set boundaries and shit?"

Despite myself, my lips twitch. "You've been in my classroom and you think I have any hope in hell of setting boundaries?"

He laughs, nudges my foot again. "You're not fooling anyone. Your kids adore you."

"Damn right they do." I wink at him. "Of course it's probably because I bribe them with candy."

---

"You sure you'll be okay?" Damon asks.

Again.

His protective older brother tendencies coming out in full force.

"I'll be fine," I say. "I have a new crochet pattern to mess up and plenty of wine to drink."

"Joey told me to remind you not to skip ahead on episodes."

I press my hand to my chest, above my heart. "Tell her I

swear on the Holy Ghost of Bravo TV I will not get ahead on our shows."

A chuckle. A shake of his head. An indulgent smile.

There's movement down the hall, drawing his focus, and the flickering muscle in his jaw has butterflies taking flight in my belly as I follow his gaze.

Colt is standing there, out of earshot, but reclined back against the wall, arms and ankles crossed, making it clear he'll wait as long as it takes.

And he has, hasn't he?

Waited for me.

Been patient for me.

Played his ass off tonight to "make it worth my while."

My brother sighs, shakes his head. "Fine. I won't trade him." He glares down the hall. "Yet." Then he turns back to me, face going soft in a way I know he's not aware of—not really—but one that I also know means his thoughts have turned to Joey.

Because he loves her more than his next breath.

"I'll let her know about you swearing on the Holy Ghosts," he says, tugging my ponytail. "Text me once in a while, yeah, kid?"

I swat him away. But I agree to the texts...in my way. "Eight dozen memes coming 'atcha."

"Brat."

"Butthead."

"*You're* the butthead."

"No, you're—"

Laughter has me turning to see Joey and Colt standing just a few feet away, both grinning widely.

Colt turns to Joey. "Here I thought they were discussing something serious."

"Nah," Joey says. "This is what they normally do."

"Bicker like they're eight years old?"

I scowl. "I'll have you know we're bickering like we're at least ten."

"Twelve," Damon interjects.

"Thirteen," I say on a grin.

Joey smirks. "Six," she adds. "If you're lucky." Then she comes over and hugs me, promising to talk soon.

"Kick some road trip ass," I tell her.

"Expect Beth to call you."

My heart squeezes and I nod, waving goodbye.

"Who's Beth?"

"Joey's mom." Well, technically, her adopted mom, but the qualifier isn't necessary. She's Joey's and Damon's Joey's...so now both Damon and I are Beth's.

And John's, her adopted dad.

"When Damon and Joey first started sniffing around each other, we banded together to make sure they didn't screw up the best thing that happened to them." I grin. "And now we talk once a week, figuring out how to—"

"Drive them crazy?"

I laugh. "I think you mean take over the world."

"Why do I feel like you and Blake and Beth are now going to be a terrible trio?"

"I think you mean the most powerful trio to take over the world."

He chuckles as he tucks my hair behind my ear. "I hope you'll use your powers for good."

"Absolutely not."

His laugh is startled, but then he's tugging me closer...

"Okay?" he asks as he winds his arms around me.

I nod. "Better than okay."

He smooths a hand down my back. "So?"

"So what?"

"So did I do enough to secure lunch...or maybe even breakfast?"

Sighing, I tap a finger to my lips. "I don't know. It was *only* two goals."

"And three assists," he protests. "That is definitely lunch-worthy."

I shrug. "Maybe."

He leans a little closer. "I bet I can convince you."

Another shrug. "Maybe I *want* to be convinced."

Hot brown eyes are the last thing I see before he's kissing me. Firm lips, a sleek tongue darting into my mouth, a warm hand on my back, drawing me flush against him.

And no fear.

No past.

Just Colt and me and—

A wolf-whistle pierces the air.

—the entire training and support staff and roster of the Sierra roaming the arena's hallways.

Two of whom are grinning at me and Colt when I look up, breaths coming in rapid succession, legs like jelly, lips desperate for more.

"Not a word," Colt growls at Lake and Knox.

"You know that has absolutely no chance of working."

He scowls down at me.

Then shrugs and shakes his head, a begrudging smile on his gorgeous face.

"I know." A wink.

"The more important question is...did I convince you yet?"

# TWENTY

## COLT

FINISHING my conversation with the donor, I shake his hand then slip away into the crowd.

Usually, the fundraising events take place at home.

But this one supports the hospital where Blake has spent so much of his time.

When they asked me to help get the new children's wing funded, I jumped at the chance to give back.

Luckily, some of the guys were happy to help too.

Tonight, Lake, Riggs, Knox, Bear, Leo, and Storm are here, along with Damon and Joey, all hobnobbing with donors, signing jerseys and posters (and in Lake's case, bottles of vodka as well). They've all also offered up items for the silent auction.

Good guys.

The best.

It might take another couple of events, but we're getting close to the Blake Madden Children's wing.

Something I wanted to show my brother tonight.

But he isn't here yet, and the fundraiser is well underway.

Frowning, I search the room one more time and then pull out my phone.

It's rude, but I'm worried.

Did something happen on their drive up?

Blake had sounded better when I spoke to him yesterday before the game, confirming the details, had promised to be here with my parents, who were driving him up.

But he's not.

And the message on my phone fucking burns.

> Blake: Mom says my cough is worse and won't drive me up. I'm trying to find another ride but on this short of notice...fuck, I'm sorry I shouldn't have trusted her to follow through.

"You good?" I look up to see Storm has come over.

"Yeah," I clip. "I'm great." I shove my cell back in my pocket, stifle a sigh.

"You don't look great."

Because as much as this hurts, it isn't a surprise.

It's just another line in a long list of broken promises and crippling disappointments.

"Colt?" he presses.

"All good. Just family shit," I mutter.

"What kind of *family shit?*"

"They can't make it."

His face clouds. "Seriously?"

I grit my teeth together, exhale sharply. "Don't worry about it. My brother...he really wanted to be here but his ride didn't work out."

"Because your parents won't drive him?"

The guys know enough to get that Blake can't live alone without help, let alone drive himself.

I look away, shrug. "Anyway, we're here. We're doing a good thing. Thanks for supporting it."

"Right," he says.

But he doesn't move on, doesn't take the opportunity to escape like I expect, like he's been doing more and more often of late.

Pulling back from us.

Isolating himself.

Instead, he shows me a glimpse of the Storm of old—kind, insightful, and persistent.

"You know I know all about family shit," he says quietly. "But that doesn't mean you're immune to it, even as an adult."

Christ, why does he have to return to his old self right now?

Why can't he just keep being the sulky bastard who's distancing himself from the rest of us?

Which, yes, I know is an asshole thing to think...

But I don't want to contemplate my family right now.

Not about the disappointment, not about trying to get my parents, my *mom* to see me doing something great, something I want to do, am happy to do...but that I also know I'm doing for her. Partly, anyway.

Also for Blake, of course.

But also maybe so *she'll* acknowledge—

Stop.

"I know you do." I shove my thoughts down, focus on something that isn't about me.

My parents are...less than what I wanted, what I hoped for.

But Storm's dad? He's a bastard.

His childhood was seriously fucked up.

*Seriously.*

"Which is why we both know I shouldn't be disappointed by the status quo."

"Yeah." Storm sighs and leans back against the wall. "But logic doesn't work when this shit hurts."

"Stuff still bad with your dad?" I ask, not wanting to poke the bear, but also—*seriously*—wanting to shift the conversation away from my problems.

"Yup," he mutters. "Always the same shit in Cedar Hollow. Just a different day, different month, different fucking year."

We fall silent and I don't miss that his eyes slide across the room, slide over to Joey and Damon, don't miss the way that pain seems to settle over his bones, making him look a decade older.

Fuck.

Then there's that.

Shitty childhood.

Fucked-up family.

The woman he wants choosing someone else.

"Storm—"

He pushes away from the wall. "I'm going to make another round of the room, see if we can't get some more donations."

"Hey, if you need to go, it's all good. You've done your time and—"

A sigh. "I promised to be here." His gaze slides over my shoulder and his face softens for the first time in forever. "And I think your day is about to get a hell of a lot better."

"What—?"

He claps me on the arm then walks away, heading for the corner opposite of Coach and Damon and—

"Hey, handsome."

Her soft, floral scent hits me first then her voice processes and I spin around, mouth dropping open, shock rippling through me. "Kylie? Baby, what the hell are you doing here?"

She's dressed in a slinky blue dress, the ribbons of her silver sandals crisscrossing their way up her shins.

"Nice shoes, Teach."

Her cheeks go pink, eyes sliding away then back to mine. "Maybe I can *convince* you to help me take them off later?"

My dick twitches and I want to say no convincing will be necessary, that we can go and I'll take them off right now, but more importantly, I need to find out...

"How are you here?"

Something drifts across her face, mischief and worry and—

"Blake and I conspired."

My heart rolls over in my chest. "How—"

"The flight to Utah was an hour and a half. When it looked like he wasn't going to make it, Blake called me, I hopped on a plane, and ipso facto...I'm here. So"—she rubs her hands together—"who are we fleecing out of money?"

I grin despite myself. "It's called fundraising, Teach."

A slender shoulder shrugs. "Po-tay-toe, po-tah-toe."

I laugh.

Fuck.

I *laugh.*

When ten minutes ago I was feeling like shit.

Leaning close, I trace the line of her jaw. "You didn't have to—"

Her fingers find mine, squeeze. "I know. But I wanted to. Now, quit stalling and show me off so I can play your gorgeous girlfriend who raises you a lot of money."

"Girlfriend talk when you were giving me shit about saying I was your boyfriend just yesterday?"

"What can I say?" Another shrug. "Double standards are real."

And then, fucking somehow, I'm laughing again.

No.

Not *somehow*.
It's Kylie.
And Blake.

---

LATER, it's after Storm has left, after the other guys have gone too.

After a fuck-ton of money has been raised...mostly due to Kylie working the room and doing it with unassuming aplomb while the guys swooped in to support her and drive up those donations.

"Lots of years spent fundraising means I know how to turn the screws," she told me when I asked her what her secret sauce was. Then she tossed me a grin before flitting off to the next group.

The result is that we should actually hit our funding goal in a matter of weeks.

Not months.

Not years.

If I hadn't already wanted to claim Kylie as my own and keep her forever, tonight would have done it.

Now to just convince her of that.

Maybe I'll take a page out of her book—girlfriend today, mine forever. Po-tay-to. Po-tah-to.

"She told me I didn't need to book her a room."

I still at the cold voice, any amusement fading as I turn to face Damon.

And I know I talked a big game earlier to Kylie about her not needing to worry, that her brother wouldn't trade me just because I've dared touch his little sister.

But the murder in his eyes right now...

He would burn down the world for her.

A hockey team would be small potatoes.

"I don't think I need to give voice to what's running through my head."

"You don't," I say when he pauses, my eyes drawn toward the entrance where Ky and Joey are waiting inside in the warmth until the cars are pulled around. "She's..." I shake my head. "Well, fuck, you know how special she is."

A beat, then a sharp, frigid reply. "I do."

"And I know she's..." I can't say broken, because despite her own words, the panic in the kitchen, the fear she feels from touch, she's not that.

No fucking way.

She's damned smart and funny as hell and has a beautiful heart.

She just needs someone to give her something...good.

Something great.

Something beautiful.

"I promise I won't hurt her."

"I know you won't."

Startled, my eyes fly to his.

"Because if you were, you'd already be dead."

# TWENTY-ONE

## KY

"YOU MAD?" I ask quietly as we push into Colt's hotel room.

"Mad?" He catches the door before it can slam. "What could I possibly be mad about?"

"That I conspired with Blake for one?" I deliberately look away from the bed and walk over to the desk shoved in one corner, perching on the edge of it. "That I showed up without a word for another and crashed your charity event."

He flicks the lock and leans back against the door. "You talked to Blake."

I still.

Because I can't get a read on his tone.

"Um, yeah."

"And you showed up for me today because he told you about our parents."

It's impossible to hold back my wince.

What Blake had told me...it wasn't pretty.

So even though their parents not showing up (and

stranding Blake, who can't drive) would have been evidence enough for me to immediately dislike them—family shows up for family, *always*—what Blake had told me about how they treat Colt day in and out...

That had tipped the scales.

Colt—sweet, understanding, protective *Colt* who demurs the worth of his autograph but spares a few minutes for a sick kid. Colt who touches me with softness and treats me with kindness...

Colt who spent two years waiting for me...

Well, it was nothing to catch a flight.

Now, of course, I'm here in his hotel room.

Which is...scary, even though I don't want it to be.

"Here," he says quietly.

I blink at the little envelope he slides onto the desk near my hip. "What's that?"

"The key to this room." He moves to his bag. "Lake says I can bunk with him tonight."

Just when I thought the man couldn't dig himself any deeper into my heart, the small gesture fills me with a tenderness that threatens to undo me and I have to blink back tears, especially when he moves to his suitcase, folds it closed and starts to do up the zipper.

"I'll just grab my stuff from the bathroom and get out of your hair—"

I snag his wrist as he starts to walk by me, suitcase in tow.

"Baby?" he asks softly, cupping my jaw with his free hand.

"Stay?"

A shake of his head. "You're not ready."

"I think I'm the one who gets to decide that."

"I think you're right." He flips his hand over in mine, brushing his fingertips over the inside of my wrist. "But I also know that—for me—I need to make sure we don't go too fast."

I should let him go.

I know I should.

But I just...can't make my fingers release him.

"Can we play it by ear?" I say. "Start by ordering room service and watching a movie and talking?"

His eyes come to mine, hold, and I know I'm not wrong when I see the need rippling through the deep brown depths.

Especially when his words, warm and raspy, stroking up my thighs, confirm it.

"You think we'd just *talk?*"

I shiver.

No, I don't think that.

But I also can't think *about* that.

I just need one step at a time. More time with him. More time getting comfortable. More time understanding the little idiosyncrasies that make him tick. More time finding my way back into myself.

Because when I'm with him, I do.

Feel like me.

*Me.*

Slowly, slowly inching my way back to me.

"Maybe not," I admit. "But I also know that I'm greedy."

His fingers flex. "Greedy?" It's raspier, those phantom strokes brushing higher, higher.

"Yeah." I shift closer. "Greedy for more of you."

Heat in his eyes, but the brush of his fingers over my skin is still gentle.

"Tell me about your parents."

He stills for a heartbeat then reaches over me and snags the room service menu. "We should order dinner before it gets too late."

My stomach growls, as though it was just waiting for the opportunity to remind me that I didn't eat much, well not really anything since Blake called and I hightailed my butt to the airport.

There was food at the fundraiser, of course, but it was the type of finger food that pairs well with alcohol—small, fussy and not filling...so all those donors get tipsy and give more money.

It's a perfect circle.

But it won't distract me from the truth.

"You're good at it, aren't you?"

His big body goes stiff. "At eating?" His mouth kicks up, but his eyes dodge mine. "Absolutely."

"At hiding what you really want. What you really need."

His hand drops from mine and he steps back.

"But it's okay," I tell him, snagging his wrist again. "You don't have to talk about it." I stretch up, press my lips to his jaw. "We can go slow with that too."

A jerk, then his hand settles on my hip. "There's nothing to talk about."

There is.

But not tonight.

It's in the lines of his body, in the concern in Blake's voice and what he shared with me about how their parents treat Colt. It's in the reality that their parents haven't come to one team event since he's been on the roster of the Sierra, even though they live just a short plane ride away. That they didn't even deign to come to the charity fundraiser he organized for the hospital that saved his brother's life more than once.

And they didn't tell Colt they weren't coming.

A lot.

All of that is *a lot*.

But we don't have to talk about it tonight.

"I want dessert," I say. "And pasta."

Relief shudders through him and he relaxes, handing me

the room service menu. "Well then, you'd better get on ordering."

I open the cover, start flicking through the pages.

"What are you going to have? Something boring like rice and chicken breasts?"

His laugh is low and sexy. "I was thinking more like steak and mashed potatoes."

"Oh, man, really living the life."

He shakes his head, but his eyes are gentle when he says, "Yeah, I think I finally am."

My heart starts thudding in my chest, hard and fast and somehow...*soft*.

For this man.

I stretch up and kiss him again, something softening further in me when the hand on my hip tightens, drawing me flush against him, when his other hand slides into my hair, tilting my head back, deepening the contact, giving me a taste—just a taste—of the fury of his need.

A fury that doesn't scare me.

Eventually, he pulls back and we're both breathing hard.

So hard that it takes me a minute to catch my breath.

But I do.

And because I'm me, because I'm finding my way back to the me that I used to be, the me I can be with him, right on the heels of sucking wind, I say,

"Then *you're* definitely getting dessert."

# TWENTY-TWO

## COLT

"WHAT DID DAMON SAY TO YOU?"

I set my spoon down, put the bowl that holds the remnants of the sundae Kylie ordered for me to the side, and debate on what to tell her.

She snorts, fixing the strap of the tank top she put on when we changed into pajamas. It's silky blue, almost matching the sexy as fuck dress she'd had on earlier, but she's paired it with something fucking adorable—flannel pants patterned with hula-hooping wombats. "Nope. No way." She narrows her eyes at me. "No prevaricating. I'm not going to give you time to come up with a plausible lie."

"Would it be *plausible* if I said we discussed the team?"

Another snort. "No." A beat. "Don't even try it."

Grinning, liking this sassy side of her, the lack of fear on her face, in her body, that she feels comfortable giving me shit, I lean back against the headboard. "I think you know that brothers will always have conversations with their little sister's boyfriends."

She scowls. "That's barbaric." Then she sighs. "And it's also Damon."

"I don't know if I'd call your brother barbaric, per se."

"No." She sets the empty bowl of her sundae aside then moves to the bed, mirroring my position against the headboard. "He's not. But I just mean I wouldn't put it past him to have a *conversation* with a man who calls himself my boyfriend."

"Calls myself?" My lips twitch again. "What? I haven't convinced you yet?"

Her nose wrinkles. "You haven't even taken me on an official date yet, buster. How can you be my boyfriend?"

"I'll have to fix that."

"Yes, you will." She gives me a pert smile then shifts in a rush of movement. One second, she's mock-glaring at me. The next, her smile is making me hard, and I'm barely able to ignore that as I try to stay charming and funny, even as the need to touch her, hold her, *take* her is eating me up inside.

And then...she's sitting on my lap.

On my fucking lap.

And I was already hard.

But now the cradle of her pelvis is—

"Starfire," I rasp, hands on her hips, trying desperately to hold her in place rather than pull her closer and grind up against her.

Because I've gone from hard to granite.

"Why do you call me that?" she asks, settling more firmly against me, making a groan rumble up my throat. I bite it back, my dick so fucking hard it's a wonder I have any blood left in my brain to form words.

Still, I manage to have enough remaining to ask, "What?"

Okay, it's not exactly Shakespeare and when she settles more heavily against me, I can't hold back my groan, can't stop my hips from jerking up against her.

Fuck.

Too much.

Too fast.

"Easy," she murmurs, dropping her hands to my chest, running them lightly up and down.

Fuck, but what I wouldn't give to have her do that while we're both naked.

But...patience.

I don't want to scare her.

I *won't* scare her.

"I'm okay," she says softly.

"You're—" I shake my head, trying to clear it. "I don't want to—" I try to find the strength to lift her off me. Really, I do.

But it's like my muscles have stopped functioning.

"I'm fine," she says. "I promise."

"But—"

She bends and brushes her lips over mine. "*Fine*. Now, did Damon threaten to murder you if you so much as laid a hand on me?"

"No," I say and it's more groan than actual word because she's begun rocking against me.

"No?" she asks.

"No." Fuck, she's beautiful, light in her eyes, hair cascading down around her shoulders. "He said I'd be dead already if he thought I'd hurt you."

She freezes, her pelvis lifting from mine, and I fucking hate the loss of her body from mine.

So much so, my hands flex and I drag her back down against me.

Her gasp slices through me.

Fuck.

Too much.

Too fast.

"Honey," she whispers, still stroking my chest. "I'm fine."

I close my eyes, exhale sharply. "I'm not in control. I don't want to hurt you or scare you."

"I trust you."

My lungs seize. "Baby."

"Now," she murmurs, palms sliding up to cup my jaw, "tell me about starfire."

"It's because you're that," I blurt.

Her brows drag together.

"You glitter in the dark, so fucking beautiful and bright despite the shadows trying to close in around you." I cover her hands with my own. "You burn with so much life, so much joy, so much fucking strength that the world could throw anything at you and you'll still survive."

Her face has gone blank.

Her body completely still.

And I realize what I've said, what I've given away, what—

Her eyes dance with mirth. "So what you're saying is that I'm a giant ball of gas?"

I blink.

Then again.

*Fuck.*

Only, then she's grinning and bending, slanting her mouth over mine, her pelvis rocking against me, driving me fucking insane.

"Kylie, baby," I begin when our lips break apart.

"I *like* you."

Her words sear through me. "*Baby.*"

"Kiss me."

"Yeah," I growl. "I want to do that." I plunge my hand into her hair, dragging her down to me. Our mouths meet in a tangle of lips and teeth and tongue, intense and needy and...

*Forever.*

Until she moans, her head falling back, her lips dropping away from mine. Her hips are still moving as she grinds herself against me. "It feels so good." Harder now. "*You* make me feel so good. What you say. How you say it. How you *mean* it."

I'm about ten seconds away from coming in my pants.

But she says it feels good. *So* good.

Thus, I can no more stop her than I can head off my incoming orgasm.

Another searing kiss as she grinds against me, her moan skating along my tongue, down my throat. But when she goes to pull back, I dive my hand into her hair, draw her down to me.

I can't stop tasting her.

I fucking *can't.*

Not even as my orgasm draws far too close.

She breaks away, gasping in a breath, her eyes hazy as they drift to mine...and desperate. "I can't, Colt. I need... I don't know how—"

Pink on her cheeks.

Eyes dilated.

Lips swollen and stubble-burned.

She's close too.

And I can give her more good, can make her feel good.

Her hips jerk, a frustrated groan tumbling off her lips. "I—"

"Let me help you, baby?"

She stills and I brace. I won't push, but fuck I hope she'll—

"Yes," she says an instant later. "Please help me, Colt. Please keep giving me more of your good."

A red haze intrudes on my vision, my orgasm sliding even

closer, my control slipping just a bit more. But I rein it in as I grip her hips, order gently, "Shift over, baby."

She doesn't hesitate, just rolls to her back, hands going to the hem of her tank top.

And when she shimmies, drags the material up, exposing several inches of gorgeous silky skin...

That fragile hold on my control snaps.

# TWENTY-THREE

## KY

HE BENDS AND KISSES ME, and it's no gentle meeting of tongues, meshing of lips.

It's fierce and needy and deep and wet and—

Then he's pulling back, hands on either side of my body, head hanging, breaths coming in rapid gusts.

The throb between my legs is at a fever pitch and I want nothing more than to sink my hands into his hair and drag him down to me, coax him into kissing me like that, into doing *more* than that, into giving me *everything*.

But his position doesn't exactly scream...take me now.

"Colt?" I murmur.

Hot brown eyes on mine, but his voice is gentle when he murmurs, "Just a second, baby."

"Is this...I mean...do you not want—?"

"I *want*."

Quick, rasping words that stroke up my thighs.

"Then—"

His mouth curves. "I'm trying to go slow, baby. Trying to stay in control so we don't go too far too fast."

My heart melts.

Because this man...

"Touch me."

He shudders.

"Show me what it can be like."

He drops his head, resting it against my collarbone, his groan shaky. "You're killing me."

And I don't know if it's feminine instinct or just that I'm starting to know this man, but the rasped-out words puffed against my skin, the way his hands are clenched in the blankets even as he keeps the weight of his body off of mine undoes me.

I lift my leg, wrap it around his waist. "I need you."

His curse turns the air blue, something so creative that even I, who's spent so much time around hockey players and has heard my fair share of creative cursing, is surprised.

But only for a moment.

Because then his mouth is on mine and he's kissing me in that hot, wet, and needy way of his, the one that threatens to melt my bones from the inside out and turn me into a puddle of goo.

But he still doesn't give me all of his body weight, doesn't pin me in place.

Looking after me, even now.

Even as the tension ratchets through his body and the desire blooms between us, he's still watching out for me.

I wonder if my heart ever stood a chance against him.

Then I...well, I stop thinking.

He strokes his fingers along the outside of my arm, down, down, playing over the inside of my wrist, my palm. I shiver, goose bumps prickling on my skin, my breaths going shaky as he slips them beneath the hem of my tank top, trailing them over my belly.

The callouses are a little rough but it's the sweetest sort of abrasion, as though his touch sets every single one of my nerve endings on fire.

For this man.

For *him* and only ever him.

They slowly make their way up, tracing over my rib cage, leisurely making their way to—

"Oh!" I groan, my head pressing back into the pillows, arching into the hot brand of his touch. He squeezes, molding my flesh with his slightly roughened palms, but it's when he brushes his thumb over my nipple that I feel things melt inside me.

Or maybe they *tighten*.

"Like that?" he asks, his lips at my ear.

I shiver and nod. "You know I do."

A flick of his tongue. "Tell me what else you like."

"I—"

But then he's brushing my nipple again and I'm gasping and he's kissing his way down my throat, nudging the straps of my tank top down with his nose, peppering kisses over my skin. "Do you like this?"

"Y-yes."

A tug drags the material of my shirt down, exposing the tops of my breasts.

"What about this?" A flash of his teeth on my skin, the slight sting soothed by his tongue, by his lips.

"Yes," I whisper, hands in his hair, all but clutching him to me.

He grips the material with his teeth, gives a quick tug and suddenly my breasts are free.

"Fuck," he growls.

I clutch at the blankets. "Wh-what?"

"*I* like these"—he cups my flesh again—"too fucking much."

"How much?" I manage to ask.

His smile is wicked and then he's bending, taking one hard bud of my nipple into his mouth and—

"Oh my God!"

"You like that," he says against my skin.

"Don't stop!" I demand, fingers tightening, hips bucking.

He settles more firmly against me, parting my legs, the hard ridge of his erection pressing against the most sensitive parts of me...

But he doesn't stop.

And, *oh*, how it's good.

I grind against him, my body moving instinctually, seeking, searching, *needing*.

And, *oh*, how he gives me exactly what I need.

Lips that work at my flesh, fingers that stroke, pleasure that grows and grows and *grows* until...

"Colt!" I cry out as I shatter into a thousand, a *million* pieces, that pleasure exploding in me, taking over every cell, every nerve, every breath, and I'm flying, soaring, completely free of any sensation except for how incredible it feels.

There's no fear, no talons from the past.

Just...goodness.

It takes a long time to come down, to float back into my own body, but it's not until he gently pulls on my tank top, covering me, that I manage to peel open my eyes.

He's moved to my side and is watching me, slowly tracing patterns on the outside of my arm. "Okay?" he murmurs.

I blink. "O-okay?"

A thread of worry slides across his eyes and I snap out of my haze enough to roll so we're face-to-face, so I can settle my hand on his chest and feel the rapid tattoo of his heart.

"That was incredible." I shift closer. "Thank you."

Relief chases the worry out and his mouth hitches up. "Incredible. I'll take that."

"Cocky," I tease. "And speaking of..." I reach down between us, wrap my fingers around the hard length of him.

He pushes into my hand, groaning, the silky strands of his hair brushing over my skin.

"It's your turn—"

He brushes my hand away. "No, baby."

"But you didn't—"

He draws me into his arms, holds me tight against him. "No, starfire. Not tonight."

And maybe I should push it, should make him allow me to reciprocate this freaking incredible feeling, but my lids are growing heavy and my body is jelly and it feels perfect to be held like this in his arms, especially as my mind drifts toward dreamland.

"Rest," he murmurs. "I've got you now."

Words, just words.

But they're words that settle over me, warm and steady...

As they soothe me into sleep.

# TWENTY-FOUR

## COLT

THE *CRACK* of the stick is a sharp, comforting sound—conjuring memories of early morning practices, so cold that the glass was fogged up and our toes went numb halfway through our ice time.

But lost in my memories isn't where I need to be right now.

Not back to my ten-year-old self.

Not back to my parents forgetting to pick me up so I walked the miles home, lugging the bag that seemed to weigh as much as I did.

Until a teammate forgot something at the rink and after they circled back to get it, their mom saw me walking, realized what I was doing.

For the rest of that season, I had a ride—both to and from practices and games.

The sting of the slash across my hands snaps me into focus.

I'm working, and yeah, it's work that's playing a game (a game my parents can't be bothered to attend even though I got them prime tickets near the glass), but it's a game that made it possible to pay for Blake's care, to pay off the second mortgage on their house they took to cover the expenses before I started really getting paid the big bucks.

And they didn't come.

Not tonight. Not yesterday. Not so many times before.

The whistle trills just as the fucker from the other team slashes me again, and the my-dick-is-bigger-than-your-dick jostling and mind games that take place before each and every face-off snap something in me tonight.

I shove the fucker—hard—sending him to the ice, ass over tea kettle.

"Whatcha doing down there, Ambrose?" I smirk at the youngest of the infamous Ambrose brothers.

Lex is new to the league, and while he's talented like all of the Ambroses, he's also got a chip on his shoulder a mile wide. Far wider than his talent allows for.

Now if he could play like his older brother, Ace...

Well, I'd have no hope of knocking *that* block of muscle over.

"Fuck you," he growls, but I'm already starting toward the net, Lake having won the face-off back to Riggs at the point.

It's not a pleasant place to be, their defense doing their best to clear out the crease and give their goalie an unobstructed view of the puck. Which means I'm shoved and punched, pushed and slashed. I dig in my skates, do my best to keep my feet under the onslaught, to give Lake and Riggs time and space.

If they're busy with me then my teammates have room to work.

So, I put those hours in the weight room to good use, and I stay in place as the play develops.

Riggs passes the puck over to Storm, who carries it down

into the corner, buying time, looking for an opening. He flicks it back to Lake, who whips it around to the other defenseman at the point. That's when I break loose, freeing up space, getting open for the pass that whips my way.

I accept it on the blade of my stick, turn sharply to flick off little Lex Ambrose then drive to the net.

Their goalie isn't giving me much room to shoot and I search for an outlet, for space to make a pass.

When that doesn't magically materialize, I maneuver behind the goal, protecting the puck as I scan and—

*There.*

The slash to the back of my leg takes me down to one knee but I get the pass off to Lake then jump up and keep moving.

He taps it back and I lose it for a second, having to dig it out from the boards.

But I manage to regain control and then I'm cycling again, grinding out some space as Storm slides in behind me.

With a grunt, I flick it over to him and he moves like he always does—like liquid lightning—squirting between two players, cutting to the net.

I follow him...only it's not to provide an outlet for a pass or a screen on the goal.

This time it's to be a spectator.

Because Storm has this.

He dekes around one player, drops his shoulder and barrels his way through another and winds up...

But he doesn't take the shot. He fakes it and, in truly devious fashion, slides it over to Lake.

Our captain doesn't hesitate.

He buries that fucker into the back of the net.

There's a moment of quiet—something that seems to happen after every goal, something that seems impossible in a space housing more than twenty thousand people, but it does.

That heartbeat of hushed silence.

And then...

Not cheers like we'd have at home.

Though we do get a few interspersed amongst the groans and boos.

I'll take it.

Because those groans and boos are fuel for more goals, for securing another victory, for keeping our foot on the gas pedal and not letting the Rattlers find a foothold to get back into the game.

For now, though, I'm skating over to join Storm and Lake in their celebration.

"Fuck yeah!" I clap Storm on the back, bump Lake's fist.

Then we're all skating to the bench and I'm thinking about how to celebrate the win with someone else, someone far prettier (though I know more than a few people would dispute that when it comes to Lake, considering all the underwear modeling he does, ha).

Last night was the greatest form of torture.

But it was also one of the best of my life.

In fact, it was so great and I'm so focused on the knowledge they're only going to get better as Kylie trusts me more and more, I don't feel him come up behind me.

Don't sense the little fuck that's Lex Ambrose winding up.

Don't sense the stick coming toward my head.

But I do feel the pain that explodes through me.

And sends me down to the ice.

# TWENTY-FIVE

## KY

I GASP and lurch to my feet as Colt goes down in a heap.

From next to me, Damon curses, then he's up too, leaning over the barrier in front of us, more curses tumbling from his lips as action explodes on the ice below.

Lake and Storm have launched themselves at the player on the other team, the player who just swung his stick like a baseball bat at Colt's head. The other defenseman—I think his name is Bear—is exchanging blows with a big, scarred enforcer from the Rattlers. And Riggs...

My lungs hitch so violently it's painful.

Because Riggs is standing over Colt, protecting him from the crush of players as the linesmen try to get the brawl under control. But it's chaos, absolute *chaos* as they work, as Riggs shoves players from both teams back, some who are trying to get him to fight, others who are too involved in their own scrums to realize they're getting dangerously close to Colt's prone body.

His prone, *bleeding* body.

"Oh, my God," I whisper, eyes tearing up.

"Breathe, Ky," Damon says, drawing me into his arms. "He'll be okay."

"He's b-bleeding."

"Shh." His hand settles on the back of my head, turning my gaze from the ice, pressing my face into his chest. "He'll be okay."

"How do you know?"

God, there's so much blood.

"Don't look, baby sis," he says, turning his body—and me too—away from the view.

But I pull out of his arms, turn back.

I have to look. I have to *see*.

The fights have been broken up, the players sent to the boxes or respective benches.

All except for Colt, who's lying so damned still on ice stained red, the training staff and team doctor gathered around him, all working frantically.

But it's when they bring the stretcher out that I can't keep watching.

And it's only then that I allow Damon to lead me away.

---

Thirty-six stitches.

A dislocated shoulder from when he fell, unconscious, to the ice.

A Grade Two concussion.

And a man who's quickly making a place for himself in my heart not yet awake.

It's been twelve hours since the egregiously dirty hit and he's still not awake. His MRI and CT scans don't show anything of major concern and the doctors keep saying that sometimes it just takes a while for patients to wake up.

But I know they're getting worried.

I saw it in their eyes the last time they came in to check on him.

"You should go back to the hotel and get some rest."

I look up to see Damon in the doorway, having gone back to the hotel himself to shower and change. He stayed by my side all night, as we waited, *hoped* for him to wake up.

*Everyone* was hoping he'd wake.

The team even delayed their departure to Texas, wanting word of his condition before they headed off for their next game.

Word I couldn't give them.

Because he hasn't woken up.

"I'm fine," I tell my brother.

"His parents?" Damon asks.

We called them a half-dozen times, but they haven't responded.

Meanwhile, I've been in contact with Blake all night.

He was watching the game, was just as worried as I was—as I *am*.

I shake my head. "No, they still haven't returned my calls."

"Blake still worried?" he asks.

I nod. "I think we're all worried."

Damon comes over, settles his hand on my shoulder. "He'll be fine."

"How do you know?"

The ghost of a smile, a tug of my ponytail. "Because he finally has what he's been wanting for years. Hell, if the man will give up now."

"I'm not sure—"

"He'll be good, Ky. I'll hang here while you shower and catch a couple hours sleep."

"I couldn't sleep."

"Then food," he says. "You at least need to eat."

"I'm not hungry."

Damon's fingers tighten on my shoulder. "Kylie," he begins. "You need to rest."

But it's not my brother's voice that's trying to order me around. It's—

"Colt!" I exclaim, bending toward him, taking his hand in mine. "You're awake!"

He winces and tries to sit up but I stay him with a palm on his uninjured shoulder.

"Easy," I murmur. "You're hurt, honey."

"Fuck," he groans. "No kidding. What happened? Last thing I remember is Lake scoring and then—" He slips his hand from mine, fingers going to the edge of the bandage on the side of his head.

"You got a bit of a haircut...and thirty-two stitches."

He touches the bandage, slowly tracing around the outside of it. "Jesus, some haircut."

"I think it looks good."

A snort, but when he tries to sit up again, I order, "Don't."

His eyes come to mine.

"You also dislocated your shoulder."

Damon moves opposite to me on the bed and scowls. "No, *you* didn't. Lex fucking Ambrose decided to clock you with his stick and you landed awkwardly."

"Ambrose—" He starts to shake his head then stops, wincing again. "The little fuck hit me from behind?"

"More like used his stick like a goddamned baseball bat."

Rage flickers across Colt's face. "Are you fucking kidding me?"

"Wish I was." Damon shoves a hand through his hair. "Unfortunately, I'm not." His gaze comes to mine. "I'll go tell the nurses he's awake." Then he slips from the room, leaving Colt and me alone.

"You okay?"

I take his hand again, hold it as tightly as I dare. "I'm not the one who was hurt."

"You look like your black circles have black circles," he says gently. "You should do what your brother said and go back to the hotel and get some sleep."

"Later. After you're settled."

"I'm fine."

Except he shifts on the bed and this time his wince is more intense, his skin paling as pain writes itself into the lines of his face.

Damn, where is the doctor?

"Starfire—"

"Don't even try to be sweet and charming." I scowl at him. "You're hurting and you finally woke up. Let me take care of you—"

"I don't need that."

The words are so sharp I rock back in my chair, a thread of hurt coiling in my chest.

He curses softly. "I just mean, I'm fine. This is the job. Sometimes you get hurt. And you have a life to get back to. Don't let me—" He breaks off, clamps his lips together, eyes drifting to the side.

"Don't let me what?"

"You already came out for the charity event. You already stayed through this shit."

"I *wanted* to be here."

"You were. But now you shouldn't let this take precedence.

You have a long weekend. You should fly home and enjoy your time off."

What the hell?

But before I can call him on the utter fuckery of that statement, a commotion at the door draws my focus.

"Hey, bro," Blake says, zipping through the door in his electric wheelchair. "I'm—"

But he doesn't finish the sentence before two people rush in behind him...and one look at the pinched expression on the woman's face tells me all that I need to know.

She's Colt's mother.

And she isn't happy to be here.

# TWENTY-SIX

## COLT

THE TRIO MOVING in through the door bring a combination I both hate and love.

"Hey, bro," Blake says, his smile obstructed by the mask over his mouth and nose, but I can see it in the flare of his eyes, hear it in his greeting.

Good to see him in person.

Fucking great, despite the circumstances that brought me here.

But it only takes one glance behind him to see that my mom is in a tizzy of epic proportions and my dad is extremely unhappy about being dragged away from whatever it is that he passes his time with these days to be here.

Probably playing games on his phone.

"Hey," I say.

Blake rolls closer, leans forward and rests his arms on the edge of the bed. "So, *this* is a change in circumstances, isn't it?"

I brace for the punchline, knowing Blake's dark humor often knows no bounds.

"Usually, I'm the one in a hospital bed."

Okay, that wasn't so bad.

I snort.

Blake grins.

My mom tsks.

My dad has his face buried in his phone, doing his best to forget the rest of us exist.

Kylie reaches over me, hand extended. "Blake," she says as their palms meet, "it's lovely to meet you in person."

"Have you washed your hands?"

Kylie stills at the sharp question from my mom and slowly straightens. "I'm sorry?"

"For not washing your hands?" My mom rushes over, reaching into the giant bag she calls a purse and extracting a bottle of hand sanitizer. "Hospitals are filthy places." She squirts a glob of sanitizer into Blake's palm and then her own and starts rubbing her palms together furiously. "Then again, I wouldn't expect most people to know that."

Blake rolls his eyes—because really, what else is there to do when our mom is in a mood like this?—then looks at Kylie. "Nice to meet you too." A wink before he turns my way again. "Told you she was way too hot for you, bro."

I try to smile.

I really do.

But my mom is fluttering around behind him, muttering to herself as she continues to rifle through her bag, and I know nothing good is going to come of this interaction.

Blake's eyes grow serious. "How are you feeling?"

"Fine," I say automatically.

He looks up at Kylie.

"He has thirty-six stitches in his head, a Grade Two concussion, and a dislocated shoulder."

"Ky—" I begin, not wanting her to worry anyone.

"Jesus, bro," Blake says. "You don't do anything in half-measures, do you?"

"Like I said, I'm good." I start to shrug but stop when a lightning bolt of pain shoots through my body. Right. The shoulder.

And now that I'm thinking about pain, my head is throbbing, the skin on the side of my scalp where that fucker hit me pulled so tight it aches and burns.

Cool, cool.

"Good," my mom says. "Then I should get Blake home."

"Mom!" he snaps. "Stop."

Her eyes flare, and I brace again. Because I know the look on her face means that nothing good is going to come of this.

Hell, part of me wishes they'd just go, that they never came in the first place.

The rest...well, that piece of me wishes they—*she*—would just see me.

As if on cue, her eyes flick to mine, holding as accusation bleeds into the brown depths that are so much like my own.

"Do you know what your brother did?"

"Oh, Christ," Blake mutters.

"He booked an Uber!" she snaps. "And the driver was actually helping him load up his equipment!" More accusation. "Do you know how dirty public cars are? The number of people in and out, and—"

Kylie's hand wraps around my uninjured one, holds tightly.

"Mom," Blake says, neatly cutting her off when she sucks in a breath to continue her tirade. "This is Kylie. Kylie, this is Donna, Colt's and my mom, and Frank, our dad. Mom, Dad

you probably recognize Kylie's name from the calls you didn't return."

"Blake," Kylie says softly, her eyes filled with warning.

"Isn't it great she's here?" he asks brightly, ignoring the tension in the room.

My dad's gaze slides from his phone at the mention of his name and he nods briefly before immediately losing interest and returning his focus to winning levels on Candy Crush or whatever the fuck he does on his cell.

(Though, apparently, that doesn't extend to returning phone calls).

My mom...well, her expression continues to be sour.

"Nice to meet you, Mr. and Mrs. Madden," Kylie says.

"Charmed, I'm sure," my mom replies distractedly...and bitchily.

Kylie's fingers tighten ever so slightly on mine.

"You convince her to let you be her boyfriend yet?" Blake asks before my mom can say anything unforgivable.

"Blake," I warn, not needing any more of his brand of interference, not as the pain is ramping up and fatigue is creeping back in.

I just want to go home.

And God, I wonder how many times Blake felt the same.

His gaze holds mine and though he's teasing and joking, like normal, I see it there—the burden of dealing with my mom's attention, the heavy weight of having to do this over and over again (the stays, the surgeries, the stitches, the pain) as his heart failed, as he got a little worse, year by year by year.

"Turns out it didn't take much convincing," Kylie says and we both look over at her. She smiles at me then turns the gorgeousness of that beam of sunshine toward my brother.

And I watch him melt, same as I had.

"Mostly because Colt is rather wonderful, as you know."

Blake's gaze sparkles with humor. "He's pretty cool for an old dude."

"You're only a couple years younger than me, asshole." My headache is getting worse and I close my eyes for a second.

But when I open them, the lights seem brighter, more intense, and the pain ratchets up.

"A couple matters," Blake says, though it's quieter, as though he can sense that I'm fading. "And it's six, remember?"

And hell, him having been through far worse than this far too many times, he probably can.

"Maybe we should go grab a bite to eat," Kylie says. "My brother went to get the nurse, so they'll be back soon and I think Colt needs to get some rest."

"Yes, he does," my mom interjects. "And Blake needs to get home and rest himself. The journey really takes it out of him."

It's an accusation.

Kylie feels it, stiffening at my side.

Blake feels it too, his eyes going icy cold.

But it's one that no one gets to address.

Because there's a perfunctory knock on the door and then a woman in a lab coat is there, Damon trailing her.

She looks around the room, expression unreadable.

Then it comes to me and she orders,

"Everyone out."

# TWENTY-SEVEN

## KY

"EASY," I say the next day as we navigate the couple of steps up to Colt's front door, my arm around his waist.

"I'm fine," he says even as he wavers on his feet, exhausted from the flight, from his injuries and his night in the hospital, from the discharge procedures, from the car ride here to his house.

"Yup, you're fine," I agree, having dealt with Damon enough when he's in this mood to know Colt is spouting bull-shit. He's hurting and tired and grumpy about not being able to do what he wants to do when he wants to do it...and that includes climbing stairs on his own.

And I know he's not just hurting from his injuries—though, he'd be hard-pressed to admit that.

He's hurting because of his fucking family.

No. Not his *whole* family.

His parents.

Who didn't stay after we were herded out of the room so

the doctor could do her exam, who didn't allow Blake to stay—as in, his mom brushed his hand away from the wheelchair controls and took over, directing it out of the hospital.

Blake had texted me on the ride home. And last night. And this morning.

He'd also texted Colt.

But Colt isn't himself, and as far as I know, he hasn't texted back.

Hell, from what I've seen, he hasn't so much as looked at his phone from the moment I walked back into his room at the hospital, only Damon trailing me.

His eyes—

Damn, but looking into his eyes had *hurt*.

Resignation and yearning and pain—so much pain.

I tried to talk to him, but he just brushed me off and went to sleep.

And then Damon had all but carried me out of there and back to the hotel, getting food in me and ordering me to sleep.

Something I only allowed because he promised to go back and sit with Colt.

Which he did, though Colt slept most of the night and was near-silent the rest of it.

This morning, he was still quiet, still not himself, but I figured that was because he was getting the hell out of the hospital.

But he spent the entire flight—Damon having arranged a plane to transport us home and then himself on to join the team afterward—raw-dogging it. No phone. No book. Nothing except his gaze trained outside the window.

Talking only when asked a direct question—like when the police interviewed him before the plane took off.

That interaction was bare facts recited, and short, considering he didn't see the blow, can't remember it, and the entire freaking thing was caught on camera and witnessed by twenty-thousand-plus people.

Now, after a silent car ride, he's doing his best to push me away.

"I *am* fine," he mutters after I've steadied him.

"Like I said"—leaving him only long enough to shove his key into the lock, to push open the front door—"I know."

"Then why are you still here?"

I freeze as that lashes through me, a sharp bite of pain.

"Fuck," he mutters, shoving his free hand through his hair. "I'm sorry. I didn't mean it like that, baby."

"I know." I tilt my head to the house, pushing down the hurt, knowing he's wrapped up in a tangle of complicated emotions. "Let's get you settled."

His eyes hold mine, and he reaches over, cups my jaw. "I'm sorry."

"It's been a shitty couple of days."

"Yeah, that doesn't mean I should take it out on you."

"Come on," I say, taking his good hand in mine and drawing him forward. "No sense arguing about it on your porch."

He opens his mouth.

Then closes it, allowing me to bring him into the house.

Relief loosens my lungs and I guide him to the couch, leaving him only long enough to grab our things from the car and lock up.

"You hungry?" I call as I line up his medications on the counter. "Doc should be coming by in a half-hour to check in on you."

"I'm fine," he calls back.

"For the food?" I poke my head into the family room, see him reclined back on the couch, his eyes closed. "Or the checkup by Doc?"

Those eyes open, fix on me. "Do I have a choice?" A beat. "For either?"

My mouth ticks up. "Nope. So? Something small or a full meal? You need to eat something with your antibiotics."

He shifts with a wince and pulls his phone out of his pocket. "I can order something."

"Colt, honey." I move over to him, sitting on the coffee table. "I'm here. Let me help you."

His eyes close, a muscle in his jaw flexes. "I fucking hate this."

"Being hurt?"

"No. It happens sometimes."

"Then what?"

He's quiet for a long time, an eternity it seems like, his eyes drifting away from mine. Then he sighs and says something that breaks my heart, "Needing to rely on someone."

Because his parents—

Are his parents.

And for all the shit I've had in my life, I've always had Damon.

Steady, solid.

Colt has that with Blake, but it's different—Blake needs so much more help and he can't exactly tell his parents to fuck off and strike out on his own, not without a bunch of extra layers of complications.

So no, Colt's not used to someone looking after him.

It makes him uncomfortable in a way I understand, in a way I can empathize with.

But also, I haven't come this far, haven't finally let a man into my heart only to back off or be the only one who takes, whose needs come first.

That's not I want from our relationship.

And it's not what either of us need.

So, right now, I give us, give *him* a little of what I'm good at. Connection and softness and...*me*.

"You know, I couldn't figure it out at first."

His brows drag together. "Figure what out?"

"Why everyone treats me like I'm breakable...except you."

Because even when he goes slow, when he's careful to not push me too far, when he waited—so damned patient—for me to be open to the connection between us, he's never looked at me like I'm damaged goods.

"That's because you're *not* breakable." He takes my hand in his, squeezes lightly. "You're so damned brave, Teach."

I lean in, and God, even with the stitches and the bruises and the brace on his shoulder he's so damned beautiful. "Brave enough to want you?"

"Baby"—he draws me down a little closer to him—"one more second of looking at me like that and I'm done being patient."

# TWENTY-EIGHT

## COLT

HER MOUTH CURVES.

Then she leans in. "Thank you."

Suddenly, the ache in my dick is far more severe than any of my injuries. "Give me that mouth, Teach," I order softly.

Her cheeks go pink, but she drifts closer, brushes her lips over mine.

"Pathetic," I say when she pulls back.

"I think you've forgotten about the three dozen stitches in your head and the dislocated shoulder and the concussion."

"It's not dislocated any longer," I say, trailing the fingers of my uninjured arm along her side.

"And the concussion?"

"What concussion?"

Her eyes widen slightly and I struggle to smother my smile. She clocks it anyway, her nose wrinkling and her eyes narrowing into a slight scowl. "You're terrible."

"I thought you said I was rather wonderful?"

A sharp sigh, but I can see she's fighting a smile.

"Give me a taste of that."

"Of wh-what?"

"Your smile. Your mouth. *You.*"

"Honey, you're hurt."

"Yeah." I flick my eyes down toward where my dick is straining against the fabric of my jeans. "I am."

Her gaze follows mine then jerks back up, cheeks going pink. "Terrible, I say. *Terrible.*"

"Kiss me, Teach."

"I already did."

"A real kiss."

"Again," she says exasperation in her words. "*Concussion.*" Her lips press lightly to my temple. "And stitches." To the bruised skin near the injury. "And *shoulder.*" Her mouth brushes over the top of the brace.

"Fine."

She blinks, leans back slightly. "Fine?"

"Yup. I'll just kiss you."

Her eyes go wide, mouth dropping open.

And I take full advantage, plunging my hand into her hair, bringing her lips to mine, stroking my tongue inside. Sleek and wet, like I know the rest of her will be, her moan tumbling from her mouth to mine, the taste of her pleasure the strongest aphrodisiac.

I want to take her.

*Need* to. Need it more than my next thought, my next breath.

My next heartbeat.

And that's when pain lances through me.

I tear my lips from hers on an agonized groan and she

winces as I sink back into the couch, trying to breathe through the bursts of red-hot hurt.

"Rest," she murmurs. "I'll get your pain meds and antibiotics."

"I don't need—"

"And food. You want a sandwich and soup or something more substantial?"

"I don't need—"

"Cool. Sandwich and soup it is."

"You know," I mutter as she gently pushes back the hair that's fallen into my face, "I always thought you were quiet and shy, not as stubborn as a dog to a bone."

Her mouth hitches up. "Good thing you're learning the real me then, huh?"

"Yeah," I murmur, knowing it's better than good.

It's all I've ever wanted.

*More.*

"Now text your brother." Her smile widens, her voice in a stage-whisper. "And just FYI, I've got bossy down pat too."

---

"You sure that you're going to be okay?" she asks two days later.

I'm holding her backpack in my free hand and she's worrying herself silly.

I wish I could say I've had a miraculous recovery and I'm ready to hit the ice, but I spent most of the weekend laying on the couch, watching Kylie's crappy—but yes, I've become addicted to it—reality TV shows, and sleeping.

And Ky has barely left my side.

She *has* gotten through a lot of her students' papers, however.

She's told me she's caught up for the first time ever.

One thing I could give her—forced confinement to finish her grading.

Go, me.

"I promise I'm okay. The guys are coming over in a bit and then Doc's going to get me started on some simple PT later this afternoon."

Her brows drag together. "So soon? You've barely begun to heal."

"Doc and Ivy have me covered, plus you know Sam would never let one of *her* players"—because our head trainer is a pit bull when it comes to protecting us—"rush through their recovery."

That calms her.

Because she knows Sam.

"Right."

"Baby?"

She nibbles at the corner of her mouth. "Yeah?"

"Thank you."

She frowns, the vee between her brows deepening. "For what?"

"For being here even when I was being a dick. For caring enough to stick around."

"Blake and I made a deal," she says, taking the bag from me and tossing it into the back seat of her car.

Worry coils in my belly. "About what?"

"We're going to get you used to it." She turns toward me, coming close, resting her hand on my chest, just above my heart.

"Get used to it meaning...what exactly?"

"Having people take care of you."

I rock back on my heels. "Kylie—"

"And that right there." She lifts on tiptoe, presses her lips to my cheek. "That's what you have to get used to, honey."

"I don't need—"

"I know." Her fingers find mine, squeeze. "But I need to give it to my boyfriend."

My heart's pounding, skin stretched too tight around my body, discomfort in every fucking cell. I do things on my own. I'm *fine* on my own.

Except...I haven't really been on my own since I came to the Sierra.

First, it was the locker room that Lake and Joey created and fostered, impossible to hang on the outskirts when they were determined to bind us together. Then it was Knox and his demands that I join in on Game Nights, the way Riggs and the others all accepted me without thought. And finally, it was Kylie with the shadows in her eyes and all that shy wielded as a shield to keep me away.

Shy that's gone now.

Replaced by mischievous eyes and a smile I want to taste and a budding relationship with my brother.

Fuck, I never so much as stood a chance, did I?

"Resignation," she teases. "Finally."

I touch her cheek. "More like relief that I finally managed to convince you to use the B-word."

"I wouldn't go *that* far."

"Too late. It's out there." A beat. "It's *been* out there."

"Oh yeah?"

"The fundraiser. The hospital. Just now."

She taps a finger to her lips. "Hmm. Have the pain meds addled your brain?"

"Brat," I mock-grumble, tugging at the end of her ponytail. "Now kiss me and get out of here before you're late."

For once, she doesn't give me sass, just lays a kiss on me that threatens to turn all my good intentions about her going to work to ash then calmly steps back and drops into the driver's seat.

A moment later, she's gone.

But less than twenty minutes after that my phone buzzes and the message has my mouth tipping up.

Kylie: I'll consider the boyfriend label.

Colt: Too late. You're already mine.

# TWENTY-NINE

## KY

TOO LATE. *You're already mine.*

Yeah, suffice to say, I'm falling hard and fast for one Colt Madden.

"Is your boyfriend okay?" My head jerks up, and I realize that the break between periods is over, my next class having already filed in as I mooned over the words he sent me.

"Sorry, what?"

"Your boyfriend," Adrian says. "Didn't he get hurt?"

"*He* didn't get hurt," Simon mutters. "Someone hurt *him*. My dad says the ass—" His eyes come to mine and he winces. "Er...my dad says the player who hurt him may get arrested."

I fucking hope so.

But that's yet to be determined.

"Colt is doing much better. He'll be out for a month or so, but he's fine. Now. Let's get down to more fun things, namely history."

Good-natured groans fill the air but I don't acknowledge

them, just fire up the projector and start telling my story. Today it's about the fall of Rome and as it often does, the drama and stories of bravery and battles and corruption and love keep my kids entertained until the bell rings.

"Remember to keep working on your projects. They're due on Friday," I call as they hurry to pack up and rush out the door.

"Ms. C?"

I look up from my attendance (I'm terrible about remembering to put it in on time) to see Adrian standing in front of my desk. "What's up, bud?"

"Will you give this to Colt?" he says, dropping the folded paper onto the surface. "I made it for him."

*Get Well Soon* is inscribed on the front, along with a hand-drawn picture of a hockey player.

"This is really good, Adrian."

He shrugs. "So will you give it to him?"

I nod. "Of course."

"Thanks, Ms. C," he says, grabbing his bag and running out of the room.

And God, that does my heart good—to have him here, to see him happy, to see him *running*.

I carefully tuck the card away, and then my next class is shuffling in, and I'm resetting my slides, preparing to talk about Rome again and all of its idiosyncrasies.

Which has me smiling and snagging my phone.

> Kylie: How often do you think about the Roman Empire?

> Colt: *almost immediately* I don't know, like a couple of times a week.

> Colt: Is this official research, Teach?

> Kylie: Maaaaybe.

Colt: If so, apparently I'm the weird one. Because "real men" think about it daily...if not hourly.

I snort.

> Kylie: Good to know.

I slip my cell away as the bell rings, get down to business with a class that doesn't have the wonderfulness of Adrian and Simon and Lara, but is still filled with amazing students who both challenge me and brighten my day.

Then the final bell has gone and I'm packing up, intent on getting back to Colt.

Only before I get to make a break for it, there's a knock at my classroom door.

For a second, I hope it's Colt (though I'll be pissed if it *is* him since he's in absolutely no shape to be driving). But it's only for a second because then I see Holly's eyes through the window.

Muttering a curse, I snag my backpack and toss it over my shoulder as I move to the door. I flick off the lights, pull it open, and step through to meet Holly in the hall.

"Hey," I say.

"Have a minute?" she asks.

"Want to walk with me to my car?" I close the door. "I'm in a bit of a hurry. If it'll take longer than that, I'm happy to schedule something."

Happy may be a stretch.

But I'm also not going to stay late just to kiss her ass.

She pauses as I wait then sighs softly. "Let's walk out to your car."

I nod and start moving, not missing that it takes a second for her to start following me. "We need to talk."

"About Adrian?" I ask. "He's such a pleasure to have back in class. Mrs. Smythe and Mr. Rodriguez both mentioned the same thing to me in the staff room at lunch today."

"Yes, yes, that's great," she says. "Though, his parents aren't happy with the district."

No fucking shit, I want to say.

Instead, I just wait.

"They're talking about pulling their donation."

Tell me that my boss wasn't so damned stupid as to mess with the sick kid of someone who donates enough money to the district that they'll care if they pull their donation.

Still, I don't talk. I just wait.

And walk.

"I might have mentioned to the superintendent that you could bring them back around."

Dread—and disgust—wash over me in a cold wave of sensation.

But I don't speak.

Not yet.

Though, right now it's because I might say something unforgivable, something that'll cause me to lose my job.

We push through the front doors of school as she asks, "So, can you?"

"Can I what?"

Another sigh, this one so aggrieved it piques my temper. "So can you talk to Adrian's parents? Make it clear how much we're relying on their very generous donation to keep essential programs running."

I need wine.

And reality TV.

And maybe an orgasm.

"I'm not sure that it's my place," I begin.

"Please, Kylie. I need you to be a team player right now."

"I understand, but this is seriously inappropriate, Holly, and I—"

"Their donation pays for library and counselor hours," she snaps. "Do you seriously want those to be reduced for your students?"

Because the district only funds a limited amount of those hours per school.

I rub at the throb in my temple.

Then nod.

"I'll talk to them."

"Good. I'll expect a positive update in the next couple of days."

Then, without a thank you or another glance, she spins on her heel and takes off back for the school.

Leaving me with an unenviable task I don't want to undertake.

And the distinct notion that this isn't going to end well.

# THIRTY

## COLT

"YOU GOING to tell me about it?" I ask late that night, Kylie's slender body pressed close to mine, my good arm curled around her shoulders.

And it's not lost on me that I've gone from not being able to touch her—this woman I've wanted for so long—to having her in my bed, cuddled close.

"About what?"

I kiss the top of her head, draw her even closer to my side. "About the look on your face when you came home today."

It hadn't been the right time to talk, not then, not with the guys deciding they'd keep me company as Doc had "tortured" me.

Okay, so less torture and more exam and making sure the doctors in Utah had done right by me.

I'll have to wait until later in the week and everything stabilizes before I start the exercises.

Annoying that it won't be the stitches or concussion keeping me out of the game.

But the fucking shoulder because I *fell* wrong.

And have now earned the nickname Klutz because it sounds so close to Colt.

Which it doesn't, of course, but Knox is an asshole and the other guys thought it was hilarious, so there's no use fighting it.

That shit is going to stick, and it'll just be worse if I make a big deal about it.

"It's nothing," she says, the beautiful liar.

"Tell me," I order.

She presses her hand onto my chest, lifting up so she can scowl at me. "Orders...*Klutz?*"

"Rude." I tug at the strand of her hair that always escapes to fall forward and curl over her cheek. Tonight, it's slipped free of the braid she attempted to corral it into after she got ready for bed.

I watched as she brushed her teeth and slapped shit on her face, as she changed into pajamas that are adorable—and have just enough lace to make me hard.

Then again, I'm always hard when it comes to Kylie.

Still, I was fascinated as she combed and put oily stuff on the strands—oil that I've only now realized is the faint floral scent I've always associated with her.

It's stronger now.

Distracting.

Almost as much as when I'd watched her massage it into the ends before braiding her hair with instinctive, unhurried motions.

Also almost as much as the smile that fills her face now when she says, "You like the picture Adrian drew for you?"

"You know I do," I say, tugging at her braid again. "Now spill, Teach."

"It's obliquely related," she grumbles, sitting up and knocking my arm from her shoulders down to her waist. I start stroking light patterns on her hip, and it's not lost on me either that she's not scared of me touching her like this.

And in other ways.

I smother my grin and focus. "How?"

"Holly"—her boss—"stopped me after school today, asking that I talk to Adrian's parents."

My amusement fades. I don't like that woman and I don't like the shit she tried to pull with Adrian. Partly because Blake dealt with that crap all the time, but mostly because Adrian is a good kid and deserves to be in school if he's able. "About what?"

She explains then sighs and leans down to trace her fingers along my jaw. "Yeah, I think that's exactly what my face looks like too."

"She's a problem."

"I know she is." Kylie scowls. "The worst part is I thought she was my friend, and I usually pick better friends. I just can't believe she wouldn't try to do better by him, by all the kids."

"Sometimes money gets in the way."

"Yeah."

"So you're going to do it?"

Her eyes go wide. "How do you know?"

"It's not just Adrian affected by the cuts in library and counseling hours. It impacts all the students."

"I wish I could kiss you right now."

I frown. "Why can't you?"

"Because kissing could lead to other things"—her eyes flick to my shoulder—"and you need to rest that arm." Her hand settles on my chest. "And your head."

"And my stitches?"

A roll of her eyes. "You know what I mean. You were really hurt, Colt. You scared me." Her bottom lip trembles. "I...you're the only person, the only man..." Pink on her cheeks, her words fading into silence.

I draw her back down against me. "You're the only person, only *woman*..."

"The only woman...what?"

"The same thing as *you* were going to say, starfire."

That pink deepens and my dick twitches.

"Or maybe not," I murmur, stroking my hand along her spine, hitching her leg over my hips. The lush weight of her thigh brushes my erection and it takes everything in me to not groan, to not thrust up into her. "What were you going to say?"

She moans softly and burrows closer. "I think you know."

"*Baby.*"

Lips on my throat, her legs shifting over me, her breasts pressed to my side.

Right.

This is good...and bad.

Because I only have one fucking hand right now.

Those lips trail up, slowly make their way to my jaw, to my ear. "You're the only..." She flicks her tongue out and I groan, clutching her leg closer to me, grinding myself against her. Fuck that feels good...

And it's not nearly enough.

"The only," she says again, teeth nipping at my skin.

"The only what?" I rasp as my dick gets even harder.

"The only man I want to kiss." Lips on my neck again. "To touch." Her hand settles on my chest and starts moving south "To *lick*." Another flick of that tongue as those fingers drift lower and lower and *lower,* until they halt, one tapping an inch above the waistband of my sweats. "And maybe..."

I tense, blood having followed her hand on its journey, all but leaving my brain barely functioning and my cock...my cock harder than I've ever been.

Lips at my ear. "...to suck."

*Fuck.*

*"Kylie."*

# THIRTY-ONE

## KY

HE SAYS my name like it's a promise...and a warning.

"What?" I ask innocently, tapping my fingers on the hard plane of his lower abs.

This is so the wrong time for this but also...maybe it's the *right* time.

To get this man who looks after everyone but himself to give up control.

To accept some care in return.

To touch him as I've dreamed of, to make him feel good, to continue smoothing down the roughened edges of pain inside me, transforming them from something barbed and ugly into...

More.

Beauty and hope.

And moving forward with someone who's...

Important and in my heart and who...I'm falling for.

No.

*Have* fallen for.

"We should get some rest," he rasps.

"We will." I arch into him, dragging my leg over the hard jut of his erection.

He hisses out a breath, palm clamping down onto my thigh, staying my movements, his skin scorching my flesh through the fabric of my pajamas. "Kylie. *Baby*. You've had a long weekend, a long day."

"So have you."

"Exactly," he rasps. "So we should go to bed."

"Mmm." I slip my fingertips just under the waistband of his sweats and he jerks. "Maybe we should."

"Right. Good that you agree."

He shifts restlessly. "Baby, you need to move your hand."

"Okay."

I shove it fully into his sweats, wrapping my fingers around him. "So hard," I murmur, shifting my leg so I have room. And maybe it's been a long time since I've touched a man like this, maybe even before I was raped, it was only a handful of times I did it, and maybe even then it was fumbling and teenage hormones and feeling strange and awkward and unwieldy.

There's nothing awkward about this.

Nothing strange and fumbling.

Like everything with Colt from that night in my kitchen a couple of weeks ago, it feels natural.

Normal.

Easy.

And sexy as hell.

"Kylie." My name is barely discernible, his voice like so much sandpaper. "Baby—"

I stroke my hand up.

*"Fuck!"*

His hips hitch, pushing the hard length of him into my hand.

So I go down and back up, only this time I feel a bead of moisture hit the tops of my fingers, and it's so intriguing, so tempting, I can't stop myself from sliding my thumb over it.

He groans as I smooth it into his skin.

I want to taste it, want it on my tongue and down my throat, but even as that erotic image flashes through my mind I know I'm not ready for that.

Not quite yet.

So, I keep my hand moving, stroking up and down, up and down, struck by the beauty of his face as I touch him. His neck is arched, the cords on his throat standing out in sharp relief, and the sheen of sweat on his skin makes my mouth water.

I want to taste him there too, savor the tang of the salt on my tongue.

And I can.

So...I do.

Continuing to stroke him as I bend and drag the tip of my tongue over his neck, the salty burst of flavor exploding through my taste buds.

I moan softly, press my legs together, ignoring the ache there, the way moisture is gathering.

But not ignoring that touching him is turning me on, that there's no fear, that there's only...

Colt and me.

Tonight. Tomorrow. For—

I stop the word from sliding through my mind. Too soon. Too much knowledge in the world and all the ways life can go wrong.

*Love* can go wrong.

My fingers tighten as I slam the lid on that too.

"Kylie!" he groans, hips jerking again.

And then I'm not thinking about words I'm feeling but shouldn't think, words that are terrifying and wonderful...

I'm thinking about Colt and how he reacts to my touch.

"Like this?" I ask, tightening again as I pump.

"Harder." His hand covers mine, squeezing far more fiercely than I would have ever dared, and we stroke him together, stroke him until his neck arches further and his hips thrust up into our touch and his breaths come in a staccato tattoo.

And all the while, the moisture between my legs grows, the ache in my belly swells.

"Stop," he rasps.

I do.

Despite the ache, the need, I would never *not* stop if someone asked.

"Am I hurting you?" I ask softly, noting his dilated eyes, the sweat on his forehead.

He sucks in a breath, tugs at my hand. "In the best fucking way, baby."

I shudder, have to swallow down my moan. "Then why—?"

"Because I'm going to come, Teach."

"Why is that a bad thing?" I clench harder, eliciting another groan from him. "I *want* you to come."

Closing his eyes again, he groans. "I'm trying to be good, baby. Trying to—"

"Right." I tug at his sweats, freeing the hard length of him. "No more of that."

And then I wrap my hand around his cock and give him what he gave me.

Pleasure.

A tight fist. Hard strokes. And not stopping until—

"Kylie!"

He comes apart, the hot jets of his cum splashing onto his stomach, covering my fingers. It's instinct—or maybe temptation—to lift my hand, to flick my tongue over the evidence of his pleasure, but it's not until he growls that I realize he's watching me.

"What do you think?"

"About what?"

His eyes slide to my hand.

"I like it." I drag my tongue over the back, the sharp, salty tang even more intoxicating than his sweat. "A lot."

Another growl.

Then he's grabbing the box of tissues from his nightstand, grabbing a wad of them and mopping up his stomach, my fingers.

He tosses them to the side, plants a palm in the middle of my chest and topples me backward onto the mattress.

"Your shoulder!"

"Someone could drop a nuke on me right now and I wouldn't feel a thing." He kisses me—no, he *devours* my mouth in a flurry of lips and teeth and tongue. A tug has my pajamas down around my ankles. Another has them flying to the side. "Open for me," he says, sliding his palm down my belly, over the top of my pussy, pressing lightly.

I shudder.

"Spread your legs, baby," he coaxes.

Resisting the urge to do exactly that, to take when I was trying only to give, I shake my head, press my thighs together. "I was trying to make *you* feel good."

"Congrats." A wicked smile. "Mission accomplished."

A nip to my bottom lip before I can reply, those glorious fingers stroking lightly over my labia.

"Now," he growls. "Spread your fucking legs, Teach."

## THIRTY-TWO

### COLT

I'M HARD.

Again.

That dangerous tongue lapping up my cum.

The slick folds of her cunt when she hesitates for only one more heartbeat before she spreads her legs for me.

"So pretty," I rasp. "So pink." I want her legs tossed over my shoulders, my face buried in that pussy.

But even though I'm not feeling any pain, I don't think I can eat her out with only one arm.

Game to try when Doc won't kill me, though.

"So wet," she says and my dick twitches, reminding me of its state, urging me to not just touch, but to thrust into her, to feel the slick, tight clasp of her around me.

Not today.

Not yet.

I stroke through her, coating my fingers and dragging them back up, circling the bundle of nerves at the apex of her thighs.

"Colt," she whispers.

"You're close already, aren't you, Teach?" I circle and circle, teasing, then slide down again, dipping my finger into the hot, wet sheath of her. "Just from touching me." I slip my finger free, bring it to my mouth, to *my* tongue. "From tasting me."

"I like you on my tongue," she says, watching me as I lick the slick tang of her desire from my finger. "Same as you like the flavor of me."

"Hmm," I drawl, slipping my hand between her legs again. "I'm going to have to watch out for you, aren't I?"

Her mouth curves into a smile I would kiss off her lips if only I had two functioning arms.

Since I don't...I focus.

Stroking over her labia, her clit, and when her head drops back, moan gliding through the air, I slide my finger inside.

"Oh!" she gasps, rocking against me.

"That's it, baby," I coax, working her clit, feeling the inner walls of her pussy flutter.

Fuck, what I wouldn't give to feel her clamp down around my cock.

"More?" I ask as she continues to move, to grind against me.

Her eyes open, bright blue depths burning into mine. "More," she whispers.

I nearly come right there, have to clench my teeth together so tightly that a bolt of pain shoots through my jaw.

Then I slip another finger inside.

She gasps, and those flutters increase, grow firmer, until it's like a vise is wrapped around my fingers.

"More," she whispers, meeting the thrusts of my fingers, the slick sounds of the strokes loud, but not as loud as her moan as I slip in a third finger and...

She shatters, my name tumbling off her tongue.

I groan and bend forward, pressing my mouth to hers,

parting her lips so I can taste her moan, and all the while I slowly coax her through the peak and down the other side.

It's only when she's limp, her eyes half-mast, that I help her back into her pajamas, draw the covers up and over us, and take her into my arms—

Er. *Arm.*

My dick is still hard.

But when it comes to Kylie Connors, I'm used to that.

---

"No!" Knox cries, flopping back onto the couch as his stepdaughter, Evie, serves him another Plus Four.

Yup. *Another.*

Because Evie Adler (née Pierce) is a card shark.

Most especially with *UNO.*

Kylie giggles as we watch Evie put a world of hurt on Knox, and there's something perfect about her being curled into my side instead of sitting across the room from me, giving me furtive stares I couldn't discern.

Hell the last two weeks have been perfect.

I'm out of the sling and lifting tiny, baby weights under the supervision of Ivy and Doc and the rest of the training staff.

The residual concussion symptoms have faded.

The stitches are out.

And Kylie is still here.

We haven't spent a night apart since she surprised me in Utah, and while it sucks being injured, part of me is thankful that we've had this time together—

"Earth to Colt."

Jerking, I glare at Knox. "What?"

"Going to explain that?" He deliberately points his gaze in the direction of my arm around Kylie.

"Nope," I say, tightening my hold when she giggles again.

"So when's the trade happening?" he asks silkily.

I glare at him.

But, as usual, it doesn't have any effect on the menace known as Knox Adler.

"Are you two gonna get married like my mom and dad?" Evie asks, dropping onto the couch on the other side of Kylie.

Her teacher skills mean that she isn't nearly as thrown by that question as I am (though the answer is unequivocally yes because there's no fucking way I'm letting her go, not now), and Kylie just smiles and hugs Evie close.

"It's a little early to ask that question, sweetheart." She kisses the top of her head.

"Why?"

"Sometimes adults take a long time to make up their minds."

"Dad says when someone is worth loving, you never let them go." She slips out from under Kylie's arms and launches herself at Knox. "Right, Dad?"

"Right," he rasps, hugging her until she wriggles free and takes Kylie's hand, conning her into a game of *UNO*.

I lift my brows at Knox, who looks like he's been sucker punched.

"What?" I ask as Evie deals out the cards.

"That's the first time she's called me Dad," he whispers and it's a rasp, his eyes glassy.

I bump my foot with his. "She loves you."

"She owns my heart." A breath and then he shakes off the emotion, returns to his normal pain-in-the-ass state. "Like that one"—a nod at Kylie who's organizing her hand—"does for you."

"Yeah."

There's no point in denying it.

We watch the girls for a while in companionable silence.

But, no surprise, it doesn't last long. Not with Knox around. "You know the guys are saving up their shit for when you're back in the locker room, right?"

"More shit than you lot have already been giving me?"

"What do you think?"

I scowl.

"Though..."

"What?" I say, knowing I'm playing into his hand but unable to resist.

His grin starts peeking through. "Never thought I'd see the day."

"It's not like I've spent the last years fucking my way through the female populace"—not like Storm—"is it really a surprise I'd lock a good woman in?"

"No." Now his grin goes full-bore. "The surprise is that Damon didn't kill you for defiling his little sister."

# THIRTY-THREE

## KY

"HOW YA DOING, KID?" Damon asks, slinging his arm around my shoulder and giving me a noogie.

"Ugh." I bat him away. "*Stop!*"

"Make me," he says, hooking that arm around my neck and mussing up my hair again.

"Colt!"

My man's head jerks up.

"Rescue me!"

His mouth quirks as he makes his way over to us. "I'm not sure I *should* interfere." His smile grows. "Big brother privileges and all."

I narrow my eyes at him.

Damon grins. "I didn't like this at first."

"Didn't like what?" I ask, still struggling.

"You dating."

"Dating Colt or dating in general?"

"Either."

I jab him under the ribs and he grunts, finally releasing me. "Both."

Colt pulls me into his side and I share my glare with him. The stink is totally unaffected, and just bends and brushes his lips over mine.

"You're off my Christmas cookie list," I tell him and when Damon chuckles, I scowl at him. "And you are too."

"No, I'm not. You love me." A lazy shrug. "Plus, I didn't trade your boyfriend."

The chest behind me rumbles softly with laughter.

"Somehow, I didn't expect this," Lake says as he and Nova move to the door, their adorable little daughter completely sacked out in her car seat.

"Didn't expect what?" Knox asks.

"Didn't expect Damon to be so chill about his little sister dating one of the guys on the team."

"Why shouldn't she?" Nova asks, looping her arm around Lake's middle and gently smoothing her hand over her daughter's soft brown hair. "Hockey players are great."

"Damn right they are," Knox says.

"As much as it pains me to agree with my brother," Ella says, her eyes dancing as she laces her fingers through Riggs's, "in this case, I have to."

Riggs, man of few words that he is, just kisses her.

"When I grow up, should I marry a hockey player?" Evie asks as she skips toward us.

"No!"

It's a chorus from the men all around us.

Evie freezes, but only for a moment.

Then she shrugs and skips her way out the door. "Boys are gross anyway."

I snort.

Nova giggles.

Ella is smiling wide.

Ivy laughs and shakes her head as she follows her daughter out the door. "From the mouths of babes."

"That's rude," Knox says grumpily as he follows his girls.

"But true," I tease, earning a scowl from my brother and a murmured, "You didn't think I was gross last night," from the man who holds my heart.

My cheeks go pink.

"What do you think he just told her?" Ella stage whispers to Nova.

"I would pay a lot of money to find out," she stage whispers back to her best friend.

"*I* wouldn't," Lake says dryly, jerking his chin up in thanks to my brother and Joey for tonight's hosting. "Let's go, butterfly."

Nova winks at me as Ella pulls me into a hug then they're both heading out to their cars.

"Be good, kid," Damon says, embracing me (this time without the side of noogie).

"You too."

"Am I really off your Christmas cookie list?" he asks.

"Yup."

Joey's mouth twitches as she loops her arm through mine. "My mom is coming to town next week."

"I know," I tell her. "Beth and I already scheduled our mani-pedis."

"Why am I not surprised?" She comes in for a hug as Damon and Colt step outside, her voice dropping until it's almost a whisper. "Just so you know, we postponed Colt's celebration until next month."

"Celebration?"

"He hasn't told you?"

"No." I frown. "Is it for his charity?"

Joey's gaze flicks to the duo as they walk down the driveway. "It's for his five hundredth game, Ky."

I suck in a breath.

Because that's a big deal.

A *big* deal.

"You didn't know?"

"No," I mutter. "What do you need?"

"The front office hasn't been able to get a hold of his family."

Why is that not a surprise?

Rage begins to boil up in my belly but I'm calm when I say, "Have them give me the details and I'll take care of it."

Her face softens.

"What?"

"I'm glad he has you, and"—she cups my jaw—"I'm so damned glad that you finally put him out of his misery."

I frown. "What do you mean?"

"They were all taking bets on when he'd finally make his move, sis." She bumps her shoulder against mine. "The only reason Damon's not actively talking about murder is that he's had nearly two seasons to get used to it."

"Seriously?"

She shrugs. "The guys talk."

I lift my brows accusingly. "*You* talk."

"Well, that too."

I swat at her chest. "I'm going to sic Beth on you."

"I gave her a wedding during the off-season; Beth loves me right now."

Damn.

She's not wrong.

Still, I don't let my little sister energy wane as we follow the guys outside. "I know she can't wait for grandbabies," I drawl. "Maybe I'll mention how you didn't drink any wine tonight..."

Joey misses the last step off the porch and I have to wrap my arm around her middle to catch her.

Whoops.

That was bad timing for teasing her about babies—though her pink cheeks are interesting.

"I have an early meeting tomorrow," she hedges.

"I'm sure you do." I shrug. "The only question is if Beth will believe that."

She shoves me. "You're evil."

"Damn right, I am."

"Damon!" she calls. "Get your sister out of here before I push her into a snowbank!"

He just smirks as he strolls back over to her. "Want help?"

"Rude!" I say, lifting my chin and marching to Colt's car— he was only cleared to drive today and is taking full advantage.

"Want me to push *them* into a snowbank?" he murmurs, catching me around the middle, his tongue flicking out to caress my earlobe.

"I heard that!" Joey calls. "Remember who makes the drills!"

"I thought Coach Kaitlyn was in charge of the offense," he calls back.

"Your ice time then!" she shouts.

"I'm on the IR!"

"Damon," she says, winding her arm through my brother's, "I think it's time to get on the horn, don't you think?"

He tosses a grin over his shoulder as they head into the house. "I think there's a minor league team in Antarctica we can trade him to."

"You've bought it now," I say lightly as Colt opens the passenger door and I drop into the seat.

A wink. "Worth it."

"You sure?"

He tugs down the seatbelt, buckles me in, my heart squeezing at the small sign of care—a hundred, a thousand of which he gives me per day. "Yup."

Before I can reply—or tell him how much I like those little acts of caring—he closes the door and rounds the hood, settling into the driver's seat. Then he's backing out and turning onto the street, weaving his way through the winding roads.

I'm so content—full of wine and food (and *care*)—that I miss it at first.

The fact that we're not heading to his house or my apartment.

I choke as he pulls into a parking lot. "H-hot dogs?"

He grins at me then shrugs. "You said you wanted to try them."

"We just ate our body weight in cheese," I protest. "How can you possibly be hungry?"

He shrugs. "You know what they say about wein—"

I clamp my hand over his mouth. "Don't."

A wink, his lips pressing to my palm before he peels it free.

"We're not having hot dogs, starfire."

"Then what?" I ask as he shifts the transmission into park and turns my way.

"Aren't you curious to find out?"

# THIRTY-FOUR

## COLT

SHE NARROWS her eyes at me, suspicion in every line of her gorgeous body.

I bite back a smile and get out, moving around to her side and tugging open the door.

"You're not about to shove me into a snowbank, are you?"

"I need two good arms for that, baby." I reach in and undo her belt. "Come on."

She puts her hand in my outstretched one and I tug her to her feet. "Where are we going?"

"You'll see."

We had snow this week, enough to stick, to make those snowbanks, but not enough to compact into dirty icy masses.

Enough that I saw the lights on here at the outdoor market a couple of days ago when I drove by.

Enough...that I know Kylie is going to love this.

I lead her around the small shack that serves up those delicious hot dogs and up the narrow trail.

"Is this where you bury my body?" she asks as the trees close in and the path narrows.

"Funny."

A sexy smile pointed in my direction. "*I* thought so."

Faint music hits my ears and I know the moment that she hears it because her steps falter. "Wh—?"

But we're turning the corner and—

"Oh, my God."

The hidden clearing is ringed in twinkling lights, small booths set up on the edges—selling everything from hot chocolate to funnel cakes to hats and gloves and trinkets.

"What is this?" she asks, spinning in a slow circle, the smile on her face not sexy in the least. It's filled with wonder, with awe, with *joy,* and it's the most beautiful thing I've ever seen.

"Winter carnival," I say. "They hold it for a few weeks every December."

She stops her revolution, gaze locking onto mine. "Why are we here?"

"Because I thought you'd like it." I touch her cheek. "And because I still owe you that first date."

She closes her eyes.

But when she doesn't open them for a long moment, I start to think I fucked up.

"Baby?"

Her lids peel back and then she's in my arms, her lips pressed to mine.

"Let's see *everything,*" she says, dropping back down onto her heels, taking my hand, and tugging me in the direction of the first booth.

Hot chocolate.

"I thought you were full?" I ask as she places an order for two of "The Works."

"My dessert stomach is never full."

Grinning, I swipe my card before she can dig in her purse for her wallet.

"Colt," she protests softly.

"Date," is all I say in return.

Her smile is soft, sweet, and then we're strolling through the booths, hot chocolates in hand.

"Oh, look at that!" she exclaims of a tiny stuffed cow, complete with an adorable mop top of hair, picking it up and cuddling it close for a couple of seconds before putting it back down amongst its brethren and drifting toward the end of the table.

I catch the shopkeeper's eye.

He smiles and we make a surreptitious exchange—cash for cow—as Kylie searches through earrings and bracelets and hair clips.

I make a few more quiet purchases as she snags a couple of items for the reading corner in her classroom, and then we're moving toward the dance floor where the soft music is originating. It's covered by a tent with tables on the perimeter and heaters propped up at regular intervals to make it a cozy place to stop and eat the funnel cake she insists she has room for.

"Want some?" she asks, breaking off a piece and holding it up.

I open my mouth to accept the offering, nipping at her fingers as she plops it into my mouth.

Giggling, she breaks off some for herself.

"This is wonderful," she says softly.

"It is."

"No." She gives me another bite. "I mean, this time with you. The snow starting to fall. That stuffed cow in your pocket—"

I pat said pocket. "Is that what that is?"

A grin. Another proffered bite of funnel cake. "Treats and

trinkets, soft music and cool air and a hot hockey player to keep me warm."

"Now we're talking." I break off a bite, pop it into my mouth, reach for another—

Her hand snags my wrist, and I start to lift my free palm in surrender, a promise to leave her treat for her rising in my throat.

"You're wonderful, Colt," she murmurs. "*You.* All that you are. All that you make me feel."

"Baby—" I begin, seeing her eyes glimmer with emotion.

"Dance with me?" she asks, blinking rapidly.

"Always, starfire." I turn toward the dance floor, the soft music lending itself to holding her close and drying those tears of hers.

"No," she says and before I can ask her to explain, she's tossing the remains of the funnel cake in the trash and tugging me out from under the tent.

Into the powder floating from the sky.

She flows into my arms like she's never been hurt, like she's never been scared of my touch...like she's never spent a moment anywhere else except my embrace.

"You're beautiful."

"And you're wonderful," she says again and I feel the same burst of pleasure, of warmth, of...discomfort as I do every time she says that.

"I know you don't believe me yet."

I freeze, the music flowing around us, the snow continuing to fall.

"That's okay. I'm looking forward to convincing you."

"Kylie—"

She shifts closer. "Shh. Don't fight it."

"Baby—"

"I *said*, don't fight it."

"Bossy." I kiss a snowflake off the tip of her nose and she smiles.

"Yup." She settles her head on my chest and starts swaying. "And you like it."

I inhale the sweet, floral scent of her, feel the softness of her body pillowed against mine, and know that it's not just that I like it.

I *love* it.

I love every single part of Kylie Connors.

# THIRTY-FIVE

## KY

I'M quiet on the drive back to Colt's house, and it's not because my belly is full of treats.

Nor because the plush cow with the floppy hair he bought for me on the sly is sitting on my knees, its adorable face looking up at me.

It's not because it's late and the snow is coming down heavier and heavier, coating the world in white and making me feel quietly sequestered, as though it's only Colt and me in this world.

"You okay?" he asks softly, like he's been resisting shattering the quiet.

I lift the cow, press a kiss to its head. "I'm great."

His smile is a flash of white in the darkness and then he reaches forward, turns up the volume on the radio. "I love this song."

My heart seizes when I hear the familiar strums of the guitar, John Fogerty's lyrics of rain clearing and beauty in the aftermath of the storm filling the air. "What do you love about it?"

His fingers find mine, squeeze. "Probably the same thing you do," he murmurs. "The clouds parting. The sun shining..."

"Rainbows coming out?"

"Yeah," he agrees quietly. "You."

I tilt my head in question.

"You're the rainbow, bright and beautiful and formed only after the storm clears."

I suck in a breath.

"Too sappy?"

"N-no," I say, blinking rapidly against the tears turning my vision watery. "It's perfect."

We both fall quiet again as he turns into his house, the garage door rumbling closed behind his car, ensconcing us in gentle darkness.

He turns to face me, hand cupping my jaw, lips brushing over my forehead. "Let me get the door for you."

"I can—"

Lips gliding over mine. "Let me?"

I can't resist him normally, but like this? Gentle and soft, his eyes burning into mine, his fingertips trailing over my cheeks, my nose, my throat.

"Yeah?"

I nod.

"Thanks, Teach."

Before I can ask why he's thanking me, he's out of the driver's seat, coming around to my side. Then his big body is bending over mine, his scent is in my nose, his hand is wrapped around mine. A tug and I'm out of the car, being led into the house...

And straight up to his bedroom.

I set the cow on the dresser, pat his fluffy head, but when I start to shrug out of my coat, his hands land on my shoulders. "Let me?" he asks again.

Lungs hitching, I nod. Slowly, he undoes the buttons, pushes the fabric down my arms, pulling it free and folding it over the arm of the chair in the corner.

But when he reaches for his own jacket, I step close. "Let *me?*"

Warmth in his eyes, a hand skating up my side, dipping into my hair, his mouth brushing over mine.

Then he drops his arms, lets me push off his coat, set it over mine.

There's something about that view, our jackets intermingled, gently folded together, his surrounding mine but not obscuring it that feels right.

That feels like *us*.

Or maybe it's that the song and his words and his care have made me as sappy as he'd worried he was on the drive home.

Either way, I don't care.

Because he's come close, wrapping his arms around my waist, drawing me back against his chest, resting his chin on the top of my head as we sway to a silent song that's ours alone.

He turns me in his hold, those deep brown eyes searing straight into my soul. "Let me?"

When I nod, he nudges me back and I realize he's swayed me over to the bed.

A long, drugging kiss as I sink down onto the edge of the mattress, his hands moving over my body, evaporating my nerves with the slow, easy touches. He undoes my boots, tosses them to the side and peels off my socks before repeating the process with his own shoes.

Then he's straightening and reaching for the hem of my shirt, but before he draws it up and over my head, he pauses, his "Let me" there for all that its silent.

I nod and as soon as the material is tossed to the side, landing soundlessly on the rug, I'm drawing his shirt up, dropping it to the floor to tangle with mine.

He moves into me, pressing me back onto the mattress, my head on the pillows, his body coming over the top of mine.

Another kiss that turns me to mush, his hands trailing over my sensitized skin, his actions unhurried despite the fire that's beginning to build inside me. He doesn't ask me if I'm okay—he knows I am. He's built the trust with my brain, my body, my *heart*. And every touch, every caress, every stroke is another thread sewn between us.

Kisses along my jaw, down my throat, the center of my chest.

A hand slipping behind my back.

A flick and my bra is loose, the straps pushed down my arms.

"So beautiful," he murmurs against my flesh, the heat of the words more fuel for the fire in my womb. He kisses the underside of one breast, the stubble on his jaw a rasp that has me shuddering, hands on his shoulders to keep him close.

But he wasn't going to leave anyway.

Lips and tongue work at my nipples, roughened palms mold my flesh, lightning bolts of pleasure shooting through me.

But the ache between my legs only continues to grow.

His body moving down mine, drawing my pants and underwear off, spreading my legs.

A tongue dipping into soaked flesh, fingers gently slipping inside.

It's slow and lazy, loving me until I come apart, pleasure rolling through me in waves.

He makes his way back up my body, nuzzles my throat, his hands still gentle, still unhurried, but the evidence of his desire strains at his jeans, presses into my hip.

He doesn't ask "Let me?" again.

He wouldn't.

So I'm the one to say, "Yes."

Because it's time.

Because I can't think of a better moment than right now, tonight when I've been loved and coaxed and held and pleasured.

He doesn't ask if I'm sure, doesn't make this about the past.

He just rolls away from me and takes off his pants, his underwear, reaches into the nightstand for a condom and rolls it down the hard length of his erection.

Then he's coming over the top of me again, my legs parting to allow him between, my mouth taken in the sweetest surrender of a kiss. Our bodies are in sync, his pace is still slow and steady, still supremely patient as the embers of my orgasm are fanned into another small fire, the flames fed with his lips and his hands until I'm trembling with an inferno of need to have him inside me.

It's only then that he pauses, poised at my entrance.

"Yes," I say to the unasked question.

Inch by inch, he pushes in, stretching me, filling me, until he's fully seated and his body is one with mine and—

"Starfire." He brushes away a tear I hadn't known escaped.

"I love you," I whisper, more tears falling, tears that he kisses away, one after the other.

"The first time I saw you smile, I knew."

"Knew what?" I ask as he settles his forehead on mine.

"Knew that you were my forever."

More tears fall and he kisses them away again, but he does it with easy flexes of his hips, slow withdrawals and steady thrusts.

Until my tears are gone.

Until pleasure is burning through me.

Until I shatter, his name in the air...and he shatters right back.

And together...

We gather up the pieces and put them together to form something so damned beautiful another tear slips down my cheek.

Lucky for me, he kisses that one away too.

Then murmurs, "Your cow is staring at me accusingly."

I glance to the dresser and grin lazily. "Hamish doesn't approve of bedtime shenanigans."

"Hamish?"

I shrug. "What else could I possibly name a proper Scottish coo?"

He's quiet for a beat.

Then I end this beautiful night of family and friendship and romance and dancing and *love* with...

Laughter.

# THIRTY-SIX

## COLT

"NO," I hear Kylie say through the propped open door, "I completely understand your frustration. I'm supremely angry on Adrian's behalf."

There's a quieter buzz of words that I can't discern, though I do hear "attorney" and "federal law."

So, her meeting with Adrian's parents isn't going well.

That's not exactly a surprise.

I inch away from the door, not wanting to intrude.

We're supposed to go to Lake and Nova's tonight and since my life right now is working with the physical therapist team, building back strength, and trying not to go out of my mind with boredom, I've been taking the liberty of driving Kylie to school and picking her up when the day is done.

I slip outside the building, plunk down on a bench by someone else who's trying not to intrude.

"Hey, bud," I say, bumping my shoulder gently against Adrian's.

Considering the workout Ivy just put me through—all of her attention laser-focused on me (to the benefit of my shoulder and the detriment of every other aching muscle in my body)—gently is about all I can manage.

"Hey," he mutters, not looking at me. Instead, he's grinding the toes of his shoes into the concrete, the little rocks that have escaped from the planter beds making soft, scratching sounds.

Well, I guess that answers the question of whether or not he knows what's happening in the classroom.

And how unhappy his parents are.

I debate what to say, know any of the platitudes I might come up with won't make a difference.

Not when most middle schoolers want to just be normal.

Not when Adrian's health means that he won't ever be able to fully turn off his brain and just be a kid.

So, I call the only one I know who's been through that.

Blake's face appears on the screen after a single ring. "Bro!" he says, his eyes dancing with mirth. "Your girlfriend dump you yet?"

Adrian jerks.

"Not yet," I say dryly.

"Eh." A shrug. "It's only a matter of time."

I shake my head and sigh, though it's with my mouth tipped up—mostly because Adrian's shock has transformed into humor, his giggle in the air.

"You know, here I am calling my brother to check in and he just gives me grief."

"It's my love language."

Adrian laughs outright.

"Is that your illustrious girlfriend I hear laughing in the background?"

"Nah," I say, "she's in a meeting."

"Then who am I amusing?" he asks.

"My friend, Adrian." I point the screen at him. "He's in Kylie's class."

"Yeah?" Blake says.

Adrian hesitates then nods. "Yeah, Ms. C is the best teacher in school. She always tells us stories and gives us quizzes with candy and when I was in the hospital she did special Zoom meetings just for me so I wouldn't fall behind."

Blake's eyes come to mine for a heartbeat and I know he clocks the situation because he turns his focus back to Adrian. "You spend a lot of time in the hospital, A-man?"

A long hesitation, Adrian's face falling.

Then he nods. "Yeah."

"Me too," Blake says. "Sucks sometimes, huh?"

Adrian shrugs. "Yeah. The nurses are nice but I don't like not being able to do normal stuff."

"Like what?"

"Soccer and go to school and sleepovers." He wrinkles his nose. "But it was kind of nice not having to do homework."

"I bet," Blake says with a laugh. "What about video games? You have time to do those?"

"Oh, yeah."

"What about *Legends of the Dragons*? You play that one?"

"Yeah! I'm a level ten mage and my dragon just hatched..."

As he continues to talk, I pass the phone off and turn toward the building, intending to eavesdrop—just a smidge—to make sure Kylie's doing okay.

But when I rotate toward the doors, I realize I'm not alone.

Kylie's there, a man and woman—presumably Adrian's parents—standing beside her...and all of their gazes are locked on mine.

And none look happy.

*Shit.*

"Hi," I say quietly.

The man looks at Kylie. "Who is this?"

"Colt Madden," I tell him, sticking out my hand. "I had the pleasure of meeting Adrian a few weeks ago in Ms. C's class."

"The hockey player?" the woman asks.

I nod.

Adrian's mom's face gentles. "I thought you looked familiar. Adrian said you were hurt and in the hospital. Are you recovered?"

"I'm getting there."

"Who's he talking to?"

It's a sharp question from Adrian's dad and I can't help but understand. "Um, I didn't mean to overstep. Adrian just looked a little sad and my brother...he, well, he's been ill his whole life and in and out of the hospital. I thought he and Adrian might have some things they could talk about—"

"Your dragon is level *eighty?!*"

We all turn at the exclamation and my mouth tips up.

When I look back, Adrian's mom's face is even softer...and though his dad is harder to read, I think I detect the ice around him thawing somewhat.

"We need to go."

I nod, head over. "Hey, A-man," I say because he lit up when my brother used the nickname, same as he does now. "I think your parents are ready to go."

"Okay," he says, but his tone is disappointed.

"Bye, bud," Blake chimes in. "And if your parents say it's okay, maybe we can play *Legends of the Dragons* sometime."

"Really?"

"Definitely. I always need a mage on my side."

See?

My brother's the shit.

Even if most of the time he's giving *me* shit.

"Maybe," his dad says when Adrian glances up at us.

A nod.

"Bye, Blake," Kylie calls.

"Bye, sweetness," he calls back, Adrian helpfully pointing the phone in her direction so the goodbyes can be exchanged properly.

I know the moment they process what they're seeing on the screen...and how similar Blake's life had likely been to Adrian's.

Then tension in the air loosens.

Blake waves. "Bye, A-man's parents!"

That actually gets a smile from his dad and a soft "Goodbye" from his mom.

Then the call is ended and my phone is back in my pocket and it's just Kylie and me.

"How'd it go?" I ask as they walk off, Adrian all but skipping at his parents' sides.

"How do you think?" A sigh. "And I don't blame them. But *that*"—a nod at my pocket, where my phone is stashed—"might have saved it."

I glance back at the group. "Hopefully."

"A-man?" she asks.

I shake my head. "All Blake."

"And you," she says. "Since I know you're the one who made the call."

She touches my cheek, slants her lips over mine, and...

I begin to think that might be true.

# THIRTY-SEVEN

## KY

"I DON'T KNOW what magic you worked with Adrian's parents," Holly says, waylaying me as I'm walking to my car the following week.

Colt is on the ice with the team today, not cleared fully for practice, but he's at least able to play with his stick again.

Heh.

We've been doing plenty of playing with his stick and let me say it's been fab-u-*luss*.

"—but they've stopped threatening the superintendent with legal action and they donated the lump sum for the staff's salaries for the year."

I'm both relieved...

And disgusted.

The Clarks don't owe anyone a donation, least of all the organization that tried to actively fuck over their kid.

But I'm glad our library and counseling departments will be fully staffed for the school year.

So...a lovely little tangle of emotions.

"—now if we could just get them to follow through on the remainder of their monthly donations—"

I stop. "Seriously?"

"Excuse me?" Her eyes flash, the question cold enough to wound.

"Just stop," I say and know she can pick up the disgust in my words.

"Excuse me?" she says again, even more frostily.

"*Stop.* We've squeaked by with this and you know it. The entire district could—and *should*—be held responsible."

"I—"

"You asked me to talk to them. I did. You asked me to get the money. I did. But I will not be approaching them about anything other than Adrian's classwork from this point on—"

"You can't—"

"I *can't?*" I ask archly. "*Can't?*"

She glowers at me, but doesn't comment further—for the moment, anyway.

"You know," I say after a long moment of us glaring at each other. "I used to think you were my friend."

"Likewise," she mutters.

"This isn't right and you know it."

She opens her mouth.

"It *isn't* right."

Her teeth click together.

"I'm out. I'm out and if you push me on this, you'll find that I'm very, *very* inclined to speak to the Clarks' attorney and share my frustrations about how this entire situation has been handled."

"You wouldn't."

"I would, and as much as I love teaching my students, I won't continue to work like this."

Leaving them would be brutal...

But I won't stay here, not like this.

"You know you don't have tenure," she calls as I walk away.

"And you know that's not why I do the job," I call back.

"So that's going well, is it, Teach?"

Gasping, I clamp my hand to my chest and glance over to see Colt leaning against his car, arms crossed, mouth flat and eyes annoyed.

"I think I might have just put myself on the list to get pink-slipped, haven't I?"

He closes the distance between us, touches me on the cheek. "You want the truth or for me to sugar coat it?"

"Both." I unlock my car, toss my bag inside.

"It'll all work out."

Turning, I glare at him.

He tugs at a strand of my hair, eyes dancing. "You said you wanted both."

"Okay, give me the non-unicorn and rainbows version."

"That conversation certainly didn't sound good." His mouth quirks. "Though I enjoyed the part when you told her you'd sue her."

"I didn't say that."

A shrug. "Close enough."

Sighing, I drop my head against his chest. "I don't understand her."

"I don't see how you would."

The wind picks up and even though I'm pressed to him, his strong arms around me, I still shiver.

"Let's get you home," he says, dropping his arms and tugging open my driver's side door. "You're cold."

I nod. "Yeah, I am."

But most of that cold isn't from the actual temperature.

It's from the knowledge that, sometimes, as good as you want people to be...

They'll inevitably disappoint you.

---

I OPEN the door to the delicious smell of my potato soup.

It's been cooking in the crock pot all day and the loaf of bread I snagged from the grocery store on the way home is still warm.

The only downside?

I'll be eating dinner for one.

I've had almost six weeks of Colt mostly to myself and now that he's back on the road with the team our time together is drastically decreased.

But Damon is my brother, was my only family for many years—and quite a few of those were with him playing professional hockey or working for a hockey team or now, being the head honcho when it comes to managing a different hockey team.

I'm self-sufficient.

I'm good at filling my time.

But I miss Colt.

My phone buzzes as I walk into the kitchen, and I push away the tension between Holly and me that hasn't eased over the last few weeks, ignore the tiny hole in my heart that comes from Colt being on the road, and pretend that my apartment still feels like home even though it's Colt's place that I'm most comfortable in nowadays.

I set down the bread then dig out my phone as I move to my bedroom.

Jammies. Soup and carbs. Wine...and hockey.

Because my reality TV watch time has decreased severely in the face of watching my favorite hockey forward.

If the old me could see me now.

Smiling, I swipe onto the text and my mouth curves further when I see who's messaged.

> Blake: All the pieces are in place.

> Kylie: How'd your mom take it?

> Blake: There were threats. There was drama. But the tickets are booked and the plan's a go.

> Kylie: You're a rock star!

> Blake: Nah. I'm just a genius.

I giggle as I tug on my pajamas.

> Kylie: How humble of you.

> Blake: 

> Blake: A-man and I defeated some evil dragons today.

> Kylie: So that's why he didn't do his homework.

> Blake: I would never lead the children astray.

> Kylie: Just adults?

> Blake: Rude.

Kylie: Yup. Little sister energy meet little brother energy.

Blake: 🫰

Blake: You going to watch the game tonight?

Kylie: I wouldn't miss it for the world.

Blake: I knew there was a reason I liked you.

Kylie: Because I love your brother?

Blake: That...and because you actually see him when he's spent too much of his life living in the shadows of my health shit.

My heart squeezes.

Kylie: I don't think he ever resented it.

Blake: How could he not?

Now my heart does more than squeeze.

It *hurts* for these men who both went through so much— and whose parents failed them in spectacularly different ways.

Different, but still damaging.

And while I'm beginning to know Blake in all the ways that matter, I don't understand him like I understand Colt.

Though I know enough to write—

Kylie: Because he loves you. And because he knows it wasn't like you were taking joyrides to the hospital and talking the nurses out of their panties.

My inclination to get all sappy on him has to be tempered by humor.

There's a long pause.

> Blake: How do you know I don't have a collection of panties tacked to my wall?

> Kylie: Because you have posters of your brother in their place.

Another pause.

> Blake: Kylie?

> Kylie: Yeah?

> Blake: I don't just like you.

> Kylie: I know—and for the record, I love you too.

> Blake: Damn. And here I was going to say I abhor you.

# THIRTY-EIGHT

## COLT

"YOU ALL GOOD?" Kylie asks, straightening the neck of my jersey.

My five hundredth game is tonight.

I'm getting fucking old—at least in the hockey world.

The players are getting younger and faster and...

Maybe I shouldn't be thinking about the leeward slide of my career.

Maybe I should be thinking about how this is a pretty cool accomplishment.

But that hole inside me—the one that grew a little bigger when Blake confirmed he and our parents wouldn't make it tonight—feels raw tonight.

No charity event.

No family night.

No milestone celebration.

"I'm good," I lie.

She leans close, presses her lips to mine. "It's really cool of you to invite Adrian."

I glance over at the kid and his parents, all of whom are wearing my jersey, and feel a bit of that jaggedness in me smooth over. "It was cool of them to come."

Her hand finds mine, squeezing my fingers through my gloves.

A facsimile of a touch when I want her bare skin on mine.

But she's here too.

And wearing my jersey. Speaking of which—

"Nice jersey, Teach."

Her cheeks go pink. "Don't tell me you're one of those guys who likes his girl wearing his name on her back."

"Deep down, we're all cavemen."

She rolls her eyes.

I lean in, lips going to her ear. "Please tell me you'll be waiting in that jersey and nothing else when I get home tonight?"

Mischief in her eyes, that tempting mouth curved into a sexy smile I want to taste. "How're you going to convince me?"

"I haven't done enough, Teach?"

"My pajamas are *really* comfortable."

Laughing, I bend down and kiss her...and as it often does when it comes to this woman, I forget where we are and who's around and—

"Give me one reason to not trade you."

My dick is hard and pressing uncomfortably against my jock.

But there are far too many people around for me to make the necessary adjustments, including—

"Damon," she says on a beleaguered sigh.

"I'm kidding," he mutters.

"You are"—she leans up and presses her lips to his cheek—"you just wish you weren't."

"That's true enough."

He turns to me, eyes sparking with humor. "You saw the news?"

"About Ambrose?"

A nod. "Fifty game suspension, anger management, and potential criminal charges."

"Not enough," Kylie mutters. "He should never play in the league again."

"He might not," Damon says.

"Might isn't good enough."

"Bloodthirsty," I say lightly, drawing her against me. "I didn't expect that."

"You've seen her play *Ticket to Ride* and you didn't know that?" Damon's words are dry...and earn him a swat from his sister.

"Quit making me crazy."

"Never going to happen."

But he's grinning as he walks off, Kylie glaring after him.

"I think if you played hockey, you would have been an enforcer," I tease.

"There's someone I want to punch right now, that's for damn sure," she mutters, not looking back at me until he's turned the corner.

"Starfire?"

Her gaze comes to mine.

"The jersey?"

Softness in those pretty blue eyes...and heat. "I think I might be able to be convinced."

I touch her cheek. "Yeah?"

She lifts on tiptoe, her voice for my ears only. "Depends on how well you play with your stick."

"Fuck," I whisper as my dick goes hard again.

"What?" she whispers back.

"I—"

"It's time to go Ms. C and Colt!" Adrian calls.

I take her hand. "I'll tell you later, Teach."

---

THERE'S a carpet rolled out onto the ice and the lights are bright, the players from both teams lined up next to their benches.

When I step out onto the ice—Kylie at my side, Adrian and his parents opposite her—there's a rush of noise...

But it's not the highlight video that starts playing on the Jumbotron or the roar of the crowd. It's—

I skate to the end of the carpet where a familiar woman is standing and—

"Blake!"

My brother grins at me. "Hey, bro," he says casually.

*Casually.*

When nearly every time we talked over the last weeks he was telling me how disappointed he was he couldn't convince our parents to bring him.

He would come on his own, if he could.

But the logistics of transporting him and his medical supplies, his very expensive wheelchair...it's a lot, especially when he's the one with the health issues.

"Colt," he says, nodding to the woman standing at his side —a woman I've only met on video chat, a woman who stares down at my brother adoringly. "This is Sara."

"So nice to meet you."

We hug then she steps back and I glance at Blake. "Are Mom and..."

I trail off when his smile flattens out.

Of course not.

I exhale, shove that down.

"How are you here?" I ask, but even before he answers, I know.

"Kylie arranged it."

I look over my shoulder to where my girlfriend—no, where the woman who fucking *owns* me, especially after this, is standing.

She winks at me, her smile wide.

But her eyes...they tell me she both understands exactly how much it means to me to have Blake here...and how much it hurts that my parents aren't.

I hold out my hand.

She says something to Adrian and he runs up to Blake, the two exchanging a complicated handshake I'd have no hope of replicating.

Then she's at my side.

"Good surprise?"

I touch her cheek, press my lips to hers. "The best surprise."

Her eyes warm...before compassion creeps in. "I'm sorry—"

"Don't," I say. "I don't want to think about the sad stuff. Not when I have so many good things to focus on."

"I love you."

"See?" I take her hand, draw her forward. "That's one of the best things."

She's smiling as the lights come up and it's fucking beautiful. So fucking beautiful I'm glad the marketing team is filming and taking pictures. Because I'm going to need a big ass copy of that picture for my wall. Especially since—

"Glad you finally convinced her to be your girlfriend, bro!" Blake calls.

Especially since that smile turns into laughter at my brother's razzing.

More flashes.

More pictures with all of us.

Then Adrian is holding the puck for the ceremonial drop.

The crowd cheers when he lets it fall to the ice and his smile touches me almost as deeply as Blake's, as Kylie's.

"Where are you sitting, starfire?" I ask as I walk her off the ice.

She nods to the opposite corner of the rink, and I spy the cluster of open seats and empty space where my brother will have plenty of room for his oxygen and his chair. "So Blake, Adrian, and I can keep an eye on you."

So *I* can see them.

So I can know they're with me.

"Colt?" she says just before she heads down the hall.

"Yeah, baby?"

A wicked grin. "The jersey." A beat. "And nothing else."

Her hair flows like a cape behind her as she turns and follows Blake and the others, leaving me with a hard-on again...

And the knowledge that tonight is going to be the best of my life.

# THIRTY-NINE

## KY

EVEN THOUGH SARA had to get on a flight back home (she works tomorrow evening), I managed to arrange for Blake to stay a few days here at Colt's house, to spend some quality time with his brother considering how infrequently they're able to get together in person.

I did not count on the power of the jersey.

Luckily, Blake was tired out by the events of the day and is ensconced at the opposite end of the hall in the guest room.

Because Colt came home, saw me in his jersey, and—

"Oh, my God!" I groan as his fingers skate through the slickness of my pussy, circle my clit in that way he does, that way that makes me insane, that makes my insides clench, desperate for the hard length of him stretching me wide.

"Shh," he says, though his eyes are filled with humor as he kisses his way up the inside of my thigh, pushing the jersey up inch by inch.

But he pairs that command with his mouth joining the party between my legs.

How in the heck am I supposed to be quiet in the face of that?

Impossible because the orgasm is ratcheting through me with all the force of a tsunami, the wave knocking me flat, sucking me under, not allowing me to surface for an eternity.

And when I do it's to find Colt over the top of me, the jersey rucked up and—

"Oh!" I gasp as he sucks and licks and kisses at my breasts, my nipples, sending me from lax and sated to desperate and needy and—

"Wet," he rasps, his words barely discernible. "You are so fucking wet, baby."

"For you," I say, grinding against him. "Only you."

He groans and takes my mouth in a kiss that's sin personified, leaving me gasping for air by the time he pulls back and urges me to my front, pulling my knees up under me. "Okay?" he asks, smoothing his hand down my back—straightening the jersey...

"With you being a caveman deep down?"

He trails his finger along the base of my spine...dips it into the slick heat of me.

I gasp.

A nip to my cheeks, the ones offered up so brazenly for him.

"Since you're sassing"—a flick of his tongue to ease the slight sting from his teeth—"I'm guessing it's okay."

"I'm not sure you've convinced me yet," I say lazily, arching back into his fingers, which are stroking and circling and—

He pulls back. "Maybe you should convince *me*," he says with another nip.

"Colt—"

A flick to my clit that has me biting back a moan. "I bet I can make you beg."

I'd bet he's right.

Especially if he keeps stroking me like that.

I shiver, press into him. "Another time, honey. I want you."

"Hmm." Slow and steady, teasing me until another orgasm starts nipping at my heels.

"*Colt.*"

Lips on my spine...

Back between my legs.

And up, up I climb.

But just as I'm grinding back against him, as my orgasm is *right there*...he pulls away.

"Colt!"

"Do you want me like this?" he asks huskily, his words hot puffs of air against my skin, his tongue flicking out to circle my entrance. "You want my mouth?"

I want anything.

I want *everything*.

"Honey, I—"

He moves, his big body coming over mine, surrounding me in his warmth. "Or do you want me like this?"

The head of his cock nudges at my entrance and I shudder, arching my hips, trying to take him inside me.

But he shifts back.

My protest is loud.

So loud he shushes me again.

"If you don't get inside me and fuck me, I'll get so loud that Blake will—" I break off on a moan as he pushes in, stretching me wide, wider than normal in this position.

"Threats, starfire." Teeth on the shell of my ear. "You play dirty."

"I—"

But I can't begin to know what I would have said. Not when he's drawing out and pressing it back in and doing it in a fierce rhythm that means I have to brace myself on the head-board, that I can only hold on tight as he...*fucks* me.

A hand on my hip, the other shoved under the jersey to my front, cupping my breast, rolling my nipple and then I'm thrusting back, meeting his strokes, taking him as he takes me and—

"Gonna need you to come, baby," he rasps. "Like now."

I'm close.

But I'm holding it back. Because this feels too good and I don't want it to be over and—

As though he knows exactly what's going through my mind —and is going to allow absolutely no part of it—he dives his hand between my legs, works my clit with ruthless abandon.

I have no hope of holding back.

Then again, with Colt, I never have.

The pleasure flames over me, incinerating any of my control—my rhythm goes jerky, my cries grow in volume (in *far* too much volume), and my body isn't mine.

It's Colt's.

It's the pleasure he creates in me.

The joy and safety and love.

My arms give out and I fall forward, a flash of worry crossing my hazy brain—that I've messed up his rhythm, messed up *his* orgasm—but then his thrusts are increasing in magnitude, in speed, until the sound of our bodies coming together is all I hear, until his balls slapping against my oversensitized folds is all I feel.

Until—

"Oh, my God!" I cry as I come apart again.

And this time, it's paired with his groan, his strokes going wild...and finally, he stills, collapsing on top of me.

"Sorry," he says some time—it could be a minute, an hour, an eternity—later.

"For what?"

"Crushing you." He grunts as he rolls us to the side.

"I like it," I tell him, cuddling closer. "It makes me feel safe."

He was tracing the letters of his last name—the M, the a, the d—but my words have him freezing.

"What?" I ask, rolling over to face him.

Lips on my forehead, fingers stroking over my cheek, brown eyes blazing into mine. "There was a time I would have given anything to hear you say that."

My heart.

God, it can't take the sweetness of this man.

"I love you," I murmur.

"I love—"

A knock at the door interrupts him.

"Um..." I whisper.

"Yeah?" he calls.

There's a pause before Blake's voice echoes through the door, "if you're, uh, finished—"

I groan, bury my face in Colt's chest.

"—there's someone here who wants to talk to you."

# FORTY

## COLT

I GET RID of the condom and throw on pants and a shirt, the level of noise coming down the hall telling me this is going to be a nightmare.

It's after two.

I'm exhausted.

I just had the best orgasm of my life after a game where we absolutely trounced the Gold and did it scoring two goals and getting an assist on a third, and all of that was with my brother and Kylie in the stands.

Fucking perfect.

And now...

This shit.

"Hey, maybe you should take a breath?" Kylie says as I reach for the door handle.

She's pulled on pajamas and one of my sweatshirts, the material absolutely dwarfing her.

And I know she's concerned, know she needs me to be calm.

But fuck, I can hear my mother's voice.

"She hasn't even seen my house before right now," I say, resting my forehead on the door. "And if I'm being honest, she didn't bother to see my two previous houses."

She sucks in a breath.

"She and my dad have been to less games than Blake and he's fucking *dying*."

"He's—"

"His lungs are shit. His heart is failing. His kidney values suck. My brother isn't going to live to be eighty. Hell, he might not even make forty, we all fucking know it, and—"

Her hand settles on my back as I suck in a breath, trying to swallow down the lump in my throat.

"He had a great night tonight," I rasp.

"We all did," she whispers when I can't find the words to go on. "And now they're here, doing..." A sigh as the volume increases further. "Doing *that*."

"Ruining it."

"Yeah." I blow out a breath. "I need to get out there. Blake—"

Needs me.

She's going to steamroll him and my dad will be his usual detached self and then it'll be months before I see him and—

"You deserved more than they gave you."

The air in my lungs freezes and I turn to her. "Come here."

No hesitation before she steps into my arms. That trust heals another piece of me and I wrap her tight, inhale that soft floral scent of her, listen to her slow and steady breathing.

A minute of peace.

A moment of quiet before I face the shit that always cuts me deep.

Then we're breaking apart, but Kylie doesn't let me go completely.

Her fingers wrap around mine.

And then we're walking down the hall.

The light's on in the kitchen and I might have been amused at my brother foraging for a middle of the night snack and leaving the remnants on the counter—a box of cereal, the milk, a bowl and a spoon—if not for the pair standing beside him.

"I cannot believe you went behind my back," my mom is shouting, leaning over Blake, her finger in his face.

God, he hates that.

And my dad just standing there—

Fuck, but I don't know what's worse.

The shouting, the bullying, the smothering *care*...or the complete dissociation, even at two in the morning.

"I didn't go behind your back!" Blake shouts back. "I told you I was coming no matter what. You just tried to pull your usual crap so I wouldn't be able to."

That doesn't surprise me.

"It was dangerous," she snaps. "You might get sick!"

Blake's face is red, his jaw painfully set. He reaches for the bowl on the table, but she brushes his hand away. "And you shouldn't eat that crap—"

"Mom," I begin.

"It's processed and has too much sugar and your body needs proper nutrients—"

"My body is fucking dying, Mom!" Blake screams. "*I'm* fucking dying. Every year, every month, every week I get a little worse. So, yeah, if I want to watch my brother play then I'm going to watch my brother play—"

"It's just hockey—"

"No, it's not!" He shoves her hand back, picks up the bowl

and brings it over to the sink. "It's my life and Colt's life and it's not fucking about you."

"Now, I know you're upset I'm not supportive about Sara—"

I go stiff.

"No, Mom," Blake says, snagging the milk and bringing it to the fridge. "You've been so goddamned terrible to Sara it's a miracle she still talks to me, still wants to build a relationship with me."

Our mom glowers.

"And I don't know what your problem is, but I do know it's a miracle that Colt"—his eyes come to mine—"still talks to you. Though, I guess he could take a page out of Dad's book and pretend you don't exist."

"Blake," I warn, even as our dad doesn't so much as look up.

"No," my brother says as he glances back at our mom. "Sara's decided that she's not related to you so she doesn't have to put up with your shit. And you know what? I don't fucking *blame* her."

"You don't mean that."

"I do." Blake is breathing heavily, sweat sheening on his forehead.

Fuck.

"Hey," I say. "Let's all take a breath. Mom, Dad, it's late. Why don't we get you guys set up in the other guest room? We'll all get some sleep and we can talk more about this in the morning."

"No!" my mom snaps, barely looking at me. "We're solving this right now."

"Blake doesn't feel well—"

"Because you dragged him on a plane and exposed him to a petri dish of germs—"

I glance at my dad.

Nothing.

Fucking typical.

I look at Blake, who's now pale in addition to sweaty.

Kylie moves to his side.

"Don't you dare touch him!" my mom rushes over, shoving Kylie back into the cabinets.

"Mom!" Blake shouts.

Kylie gasps, clutching her hip. "I think we all need to calm down."

I move to her side, hand brushing hers away, rubbing at the spot that has to hurt. "Baby," I begin, apologies bubbling up.

"I'm okay," she whispers. "But Blake isn't." She nods at my brother.

"Tell her," Blake rasps.

I frown, and when Kylie nudges me, I move closer, boxing my mom out so I can hear him properly and ignore her nonstop blustering. "Tell who what?"

"Tell Mom what she did to you."

I rock back on my heels, heart pounding. "It doesn't matter."

He squeezes my hand. Hard. "It does."

"She won't listen."

"But you need to tell her anyway."

He holds my eyes and I sigh. "Giving advice to your big brother?"

"It's my prerogative as the younger and more good-looking sibling." He squeezes again. "*Tell* her. I need you to tell her."

That gets me, likely in the way he knew it would.

So, I nod.

And then I turn to my mom.

She won't hear me, not really. The words, my life, it will always be background noise to her.

"I need you to stop and listen to me." Her eyes flash and she shoves at my chest, but I don't move. And I don't stop talking. Because Blake needs this...and I guess, some part of me needs it too. "Do you understand how you've nearly broken both of us? Do you understand that your obsession with Blake's health makes it almost impossible for him to live a full life?"

"He needs—"

"To *live,* Mom. To take pleasure in what he can do. Not what he can't. And you need to get a fucking life." Before she can reply, I go on, "Your life can't be living for him—"

"I don't—"

"Tell me one thing you've done in the last two decades that hasn't involved Blake."

Her mouth snaps closed, eyes flashing.

"You certainly don't have any hobbies or any friends. Fuck, Dad has spent most of those years—when he's graced us with his presence, that is—checked out."

"Frank," she snaps.

But my dad barely lifts his head from his phone. "What?"

She glares. "Say something!"

"Respect your mother," he replies dutifully.

Then looks right back at his phone.

My mom makes a sound of fury, but I'm not done.

Blake's right.

It's beyond time.

"You smothered him and neglected me. You can barely look at me, can barely acknowledge my presence. I spent most of my life desperate for you to pay attention to me, to fucking love me, and it hurts, Mom. It hurts that you can't seem to do the bare fucking minimum."

I exhale, shove down the vitriol that wants to escape.

I won't be that person.

No, I'll be better.

"That's done. *I'm* done. I get you have no interest in my

life. That's...well, it's not fucking fine because you were supposed to be my parent, but I'm going to find a way to be okay with it because I'm an adult and I don't want to keep living with this goddamned hole inside me." I rub at my chest, at the ache that's still there, but an ache I know is going to fade.

Because I'm building something better.

"The only thing I want to know," I say, "is how you could do that to a kid."

The room goes quiet, so quiet I can hear the soft *whoosh* of Blake's oxygen.

"How, Mom?" I press when she doesn't answer.

A shake of her head.

"How?" I ask again. "Just tell me ho—"

"Because I didn't want you!" she screams and I jerk back at the tone, at the words, at the utter hate in her eyes. "I didn't want you and that bastard put you in me and you're lucky I decided to keep you at all because I sure as hell didn't *have* to!" She glares at my father. "But Frank said I should because the two of us couldn't get pregnant, so it was a *gift*." She sneers the last.

My head starts spinning and I have to dig my toes into the floor to keep myself upright.

"And then I did have my baby—*my* baby." She looks at Blake, who's gone even paler. "Not the one that monster forced in me, the one I was forced to keep...but mine, and he was sick, and I knew God was telling me that I needed to put all of my care into him, needed to love him with everything I am."

Her eyes lock back onto mine and I brace.

But bracing doesn't do me one lick of good.

"How could I do it, you ask?" She comes closer, jabbing her finger into my chest, the look in her eyes so cold a chill skates down my spine. "Because I hate you. And I *always* will. And I will *never* forgive you for being here, for being perfect when *my* baby is—"

"Donna—"

But I don't get a chance to process that my dad actually sounds like he's paying attention for once, that his tone is sharp, that he finally succeeds in getting my mom to shut the fuck up.

Because Kylie gasps.

And Blake...

*Fuck.*

Well, I turn just in time to watch my brother have a seizure.

# FORTY-ONE

## KY

HOURS LATER, sitting in the hospital's waiting room, I glance over at Colt, still reeling from his mother's words and at a complete and total loss as what to do.

His mother said...

God, she'd *said.*

So many awful things, but it's the—

*I hate you. And I always will.*

That continues running on repeat through my mind.

Those words had struck my heart like bullets, and they weren't even directed at me.

Just...at the man I love.

Who's standing in the corner with his hands braced on the wall.

Not looking at anyone. Not talking to anyone.

"He looks..."

"I know," I whisper to Damon, who's just come in and sat in the chair next to mine, Joey dropping into the one on his other side. "I don't...his mom, she was really, really horrible." Even now my eyes burn, my throat gets tight. "I don't know how he's still standing."

Especially after the chaos of that kitchen.

Blake's too-skinny body so stiff, his teeth clamped together so tightly he'd bitten his tongue and blood had poured out of his mouth. His eyes unseeing, his hands clenching and unclenching, his neck at the wrong angle and...

The ambulance coming.

The silent ride to the hospital.

And now the wait.

Their parents—if that's what you can call them—were called back a few minutes ago, so I hope that means everything is fine with Blake—or *will* be fine.

Except, how can it?

Sara was a wreck when I called her.

Colt is destroyed by cruel words.

And Blake's body has been through so, so much.

I blink rapidly.

I will not cry. I will *not*.

Damon slides his arm around my shoulders.

"Don't," I whisper. "I can't fall apart. Colt needs me to be—"

My brother removes his arm but doesn't back off. Instead, he shifts, cupping my jaw. "He needs you to be you. *Just* you."

"I don't know if that's enough." My lungs hitch, a sob rising in my throat. "His mom...she was raped too and Colt's dad, or I guess not his *dad* because—" I break off, bite my bottom lip, but someone I manage to tell him the rest.

That Colt was the result of an act of violence.

That his mother shared that truth with him, inflicting a wound I'm not sure will ever heal.

*Ever.*

My brother's hand slips from my chin to drop into his lap, head falling forward, soft curse sliding through the air. "Fuck, what a mess."

He's quiet, but only for a moment.

Then his arm comes back around my shoulders. "He healed something in you, kid. Something I couldn't. Something *time* couldn't."

My brother had known.

*Of course* he'd known.

"You were existing before, Ky. Doing a fucking great job of pretending to the rest of the world, and"—he leans close—"sometimes I think to yourself too."

He's not wrong.

*Of course* he's not wrong.

"He pulled you out. Helped you become *you* again. If he hadn't..." His mouth quirks. "He'd be traded."

"The protective big brother to the end."

A shrug, his big hand encouraging me up to my feet. "It's my job."

"It's really not. But," I add before he can protest, "I love you even more because you think it is."

"Love you too, kid. And, Ky?"

I pause.

"Remember. Just be you. That's all he needs."

Bolstered, I lift my chin and walk toward Colt.

Storm is beside him, looking pensive, his eyes filled with shadows I suspect are trying to mask his own demons.

I don't know him super well, always kept a bit of distance between us because...well, because before Colt, I was broken.

And also because my brother is married to the woman he loves.

Storm pushes off the wall, meets me halfway.

"You got him?"

I nod.

"Good."

I start to move past him but he catches my arm. "Ky?"

I lift my brows.

"That wound's been festering for a long time. It—" His gaze slides from mine, and I can't miss that it's gone to Joey and Damon, same as I don't miss the flicker of hurt deepening the shadows in his old-soul eyes. "He's hurting. Don't let him push you away, huh? No matter what it takes."

He doesn't wait for an answer, dropping my arm, and walking out of the waiting room.

And I don't know why...

But I just have the sense that I may not see him again.

Shaking that off, I move to Colt.

Only, the moment I lay my hand on his back, curl into his side, the doors to the waiting room burst open and suddenly his mother is there, storming over to Colt, getting in his face.

I react without thinking, putting my body between them.

Not that it seems to matter.

Donna Madden only has eyes for her eldest child.

"This is your fault. And I will never, ever forgive you."

I press myself to Colt, and he wraps an arm around my middle, pulling me behind him, just as—

*Crack!*

The sound of her palm hitting Colt's cheek is gunshot loud in the quiet room.

And suddenly everyone is moving at once.

Damon's there, shoving Donna back.

Several security guards burst into the room, grabbing her and escorting her out.

Joey appears by my side, asking if we're okay.

Frank follows after his shouting wife without so much as looking at the destruction she's wreaked.

And a doctor is in front of us, quietly saying that Blake wants to see his brother.

Everyone's moved...except Colt.

"Honey," I say.

Still not moving, just frozen in place with a bright red mark on his cheek.

"Colt."

Nothing.

I suck in a breath, release it.

Then I touch his chest.

"Honey, Blake needs you."

And finally, *finally* he unsticks, moving toward the double doors the doctor came out of.

"Are you Kylie?" the doctor asks.

I tear my eyes from Colt's retreating back and focus on the slender woman with the ink-black hair. "Yes, I am."

"Blake wanted me to bring you too."

My heart squeezes, but I nod, follow her through the doors, pausing only to glance over at Joey and Damon, both of whom give me encouraging—albeit small—smiles before I head into the hall, hurrying to catch up with Colt, my stomach twisting slightly when he doesn't look at me, doesn't acknowledge me, doesn't *touch* me.

But I know it's not because of something I've done. It's the weight of those words that tore open a wound that never truly healed. It's the hate in the eyes of a woman who was supposed to love him. It's the violence of the moment and the loss of a slender thread of hope and...

It's worry for a brother who means the world to him.

The doctor indicates a room and we push inside.

"Hey, bro," Blake croaks, and it takes everything in me to keep my expression neutral. Because, hell, he's so damned pale and hooked up to so many tubes—though he quickly proves his humor is intact. "It wasn't my intention to swap places with you, but you know me, always an attention whore."

Laughter bubbles up in my chest, but I swallow it down, follow Colt over to his side.

"Pretty girl in my room," he says when I touch his hand, sink down into the chair next to his bed. "Better watch out, bro. May have to steal your girl—" He breaks off on a cough that sends the monitors going crazy and the nurses swarming into the room.

They push medication, make notes on his charts, call the doctor, and admonish him to take it easy.

"Can't take it any easier than lying in bed."

"Try. We need time for the new regimen of meds to start working."

A nod.

She smiles at him then at us before slipping from the room.

"Well, never had a seizure before," Blake says into the silence that follows. "That was fun."

Colt spins and moves to the wall, rearing back and punching it in a brutal show of aggression.

I gasp and he rotates back, his knuckles bloody, dripping onto the floor.

"Honey," I begin.

"This is *not* a fucking joke, Blake. This is your life and you could have died—"

Blake's smile fades. "Newsflash, bro," he says in a hard tone I haven't heard from him before. "I could have died a *lot* of times over the last few years. I could die tomorrow. *Tonight.* So if I want to fucking joke, if it's the way I cope with the fact that this shit"—he waves a tube-laden hand around the room—"then you're just going to have to deal."

Colt's chin drops forward. "You're right. I'm sorry."

More silence.

I squeeze Blake's shoulder then move into the bathroom, grabbing a wad of paper towels.

But when I press them to Colt's cut knuckles, he pulls back, avoiding my eyes.

Avoiding *Blake's* eyes.

"I'll go take care of this," he says, heading for the door.

That's not why he's leaving.

I can see it in the lines of his body, in his stiff, jerky movements.

He's not going to see a nurse about his bloodied knuckles.

He's finally hit his limit and...he's running.

Because the trickle of blood on his hand is nothing compared to the internal hemorrhaging that's been inflicted on him over the last few hours.

"Bro," Blake says.

"I'll be back," Colt mutters, yanking open the door.

"Honey—"

The door shuts behind him.

Damn.

Blake's eyes come back to mine. "Ky?"

"Yeah, sweetheart?" I ask, smoothing back his hair, tamping down on the urge to run after his stubborn brother.

For a few seconds, anyway.

"I know you and Colt are new but..." He pauses, a question in his eyes, and suddenly I understand exactly why Donna's rage in the waiting room was so acute...and so fiercely directed at Colt. "Do you think I could—?"

"Yes," I say. "You don't even have to ask. You want to live here, live with us"—because that's where Colt and I are heading, even if the man I love isn't thinking straight in this moment —"but right now—" I hitch my head to the door.

His gaze tells me he saw Colt's panic too. "Go take care of him." A half smile. "I'll be here when you get back."

I kiss his forehead. "Rest, I'll be back soon."

Straightening, I swipe something off the rolling table by his bed and head to the nurse's station.

As suspected, Colt didn't stop, but they point me in the direction of the stairwell in which he disappeared.

I sprint down the steps as fast as I dare, bursting out into the parking lot, the cold of the early morning a shock to my senses.

It steals my breath, but my eyes are working fine.

And what I see makes my heart twist.

Colt is getting into his car.

I rush across the lot, grip the scissors I stole from Blake's table...

And I jab them into the tire.

# FORTY-TWO

## COLT

I SENSE movement out of the corner of my eye, but I'm not thinking straight enough to react before the *hiss* of air reaches my ears.

I push against the door I'd been swinging shut, stopping it from closing, and glance out through the opening—

To see Kylie straightening from my back tire, a pair of scissors in her hand.

"What the fuck are you doing?" I snap, getting out of the driver's seat.

She shoves the scissors in her pocket and moves toward me, jabbing me in the chest with her finger. "First of all, don't you dare take that tone with me."

I rock back slightly, *her* tone cutting through the tornado of emotions and thoughts that have been twisting through my mind, gathering strength over the last hours until I'm trapped in the middle of the violent maelstrom, unable to think, barely able to see, hardly able to *feel* over the noise.

Except...she's launching herself at me, wrapping her arms tightly around my middle.

"Second, I'm here," she whispers. "And I'm not going anywhere."

My mind is still in that storm, still barely functioning.

But her body against mine, her scent in my nose, those words in my ears, and the wind quiets a bit.

"I'm here," she says again.

And it's like the dam breaks.

Shuddering, I bend and bury my face in her hair, inhaling the scent of her. I wrap my arms around her waist and haul her against me. Soft curves, floral notes, gentle words stitching up the edges of the big, gaping wound inside me.

It's still bleeding.

And I know it will take a long time to heal over—maybe it won't *ever* completely go away.

But I'm not alone.

"She was raped," I whisper, my eyes burning, and goddamn it, I feel like a fucking baby, but a tear slips out, soaking into the dark silk of her hair.

"I'm sorry that was done to her," she whispers back. "You know how much I am. But that also has absolutely no bearing on the wonderful person you are."

That flays me open and I clench my eyes closed—maybe if I can just shut them tightly enough it'll stop the flow of tears.

Newsflash, it doesn't fucking work.

But Kylie doesn't make me feel like a pathetic, sniveling coward, doesn't push me away, doesn't tell me to stop crying. All she does is shift our positions, pulling my head onto her shoulder until I get myself together.

"Sorry," I rasp what feels like an eternity later, drawing back and scrubbing my hands over my face. "I—"

She pulls them free, cups my cheeks, forces my eyes to hers. "Don't you dare apologize."

"I—"

But I can't finish the sentence.

Because I don't know *how* to finish the sentence.

I shouldn't be crying. I shouldn't care. I shouldn't be hurt. I shouldn't feel scared or devastated or completely untethered in a world I suddenly don't know...

But I *do* feel all of those things.

"You're allowed to have emotions. You're allowed to be hurt. I know what it's like, at least part of what she went through, but she decided to bring you into this world, and you deserved more than the neglect and emotional abuse, the cold disdain"—I try to turn away but she forces my gaze to stay on hers—"You're her *baby,* and if she couldn't be a parent to you, she should have freed you to find that with another family, another mother."

Those words hit me hard, draw those stitches a little tighter.

Because she's right.

"And don't get me started on your father. He's checked out, letting her pull her shit, and all he can say is '*Respect your mother?*' That's bullshit and as pathetic as the scenes she seems to live to make." She traces her fingers over the cheek my mother slapped. "It was abuse, all of it, and he didn't step in when he should have—not today, not in the months I've known you, and clearly not while you were growing up. That's just as evil."

"Baby," I begin.

Still hurting.

Still feeling raw inside.

But not bleeding out from internal injuries.

"I won't let her do it again," she growls. "I swear if she puts her hands on you again, I'll..." Her eyes flash with fury. "I'll show her the meaning of a slap. *She'll* be the one with the red mark on her cheek and it won't be small and—"

"God, I love you."

"—I don't care if she presses charges, don't care if I go to jail—"

"Starfire." I slide my hand up her back, into her hair.

"It will be worth it—"

"Teach, take a breath."

"—because she needs a taste of her own medicine and Blake needs space so he can live his life. Oh," she adds her face changing, softening. "He's going to move in with us. He asked and I said it was okay."

"Baby—"

"And I know it's presumptuous to say *us* because we're still new, but we've spent every night since Utah together—well, every night you've been in town, that is—and I don't want that to change and—"

Fuck it.

I tilt back her head, press my lips to hers.

And I kiss her with all that I'm feeling—the pain and devastation, the love I have for this woman who's never hurt me and would fight those who do. I kiss her with the need I always have when she's near, the joy she brings to my life, the careful way she cradles my heart.

Not just taking.

But giving back so, so much.

"I'm okay," I say when we break apart, lungs heaving.

"Colt—"

"Okay," I repeat before she can go on another rant. "I'm hurt—of course I am. I...I don't understand if she felt that way... why keep me?" I shake my head, sigh. "It's a mess and I know I'm going to need help figuring this shit out, but..."

"What?" she asks when I don't go on.

"But it's almost a relief, I guess."

Her eyes go wide.

"I finally know the truth of why she hates me, and I guess some part of me even understands it." I sigh, smooth back her hair. "So, yeah, I know healing from this isn't going to be smooth sailing, but...do I want Blake to live with us—yes, *us?* Absolutely. Do I want you to move in with me? Also, absolutely. Do I want to build a life where we're happy, so damned happy I don't think of what was missing from the woman who was supposed to love me? Yes, of course I do."

She sniffs. "I want that too."

"Good." I smile. "Because I want babies with your eyes and to help you grade papers and decorate your classroom. I want to find a way to get Holly fired and see Adrian graduate from high school and kick ass in life. I want you, Teach, forever and always. Not just because you're smart and beautiful and *mine* but because you see me and you love me, and you show me that."

"Colt," she whispers, tears slipping from the corners of her eyes.

"I knew I wanted you from that first smile, knew I would find a way to make the shadows in your eyes disappear. I knew I had to make sure you were no longer scared when I was near. Because I knew I needed you in my life forever." I kiss away her tears. "But I didn't know it could be like this, could be more, that you—only *you*, starfire—could make my pain go away. Ever since I was a kid I had to find a way to just be okay, to bury the hurt, to put one foot in front of the other and move on. But you" —I cup her jaw—"*you* love me."

"I do," she says, her hand settling over my chest.

"And you don't care if I'm not okay—" Frowning, she opens her mouth, but I gently place a finger over her lips, pausing her rebuttal of those words. "You love me—okay or not, happy or sad or indifferent, hockey player or teacher's assistant or newly crowned reality TV buff."

"I do," she says again. "Because you're that for me too."

"I know." I touch her cheek. "Because *you* taught me that's what love should be."

A soft smile. "You're going to make me cry again."

"That's okay. I'll hold you until you're done then kiss your tears away all over again."

She sniffs.

I tug her close, hold her tight.

"I just have one question," she says long, *long* minutes later when we've finally managed to pull apart.

I take her hand, draw her back to the hospital, back to my brother, back to make arrangements that are going to change all of our lives...and do it for the better.

"What's that?" I ask, as we reach the entrance.

Her smile seals the wound inside me a few more millimeters.

Her mischievous question a couple more.

"Who's changing the tire?"

# EPILOGUE

## KY, A FEW MONTHS LATER, RIGHT AT THE TRADE DEADLINE

I STARE AT MY BROTHER. "You're kidding me."

He sighs, reclining back on the couch. "It was a trade I had to make. You know it."

Dread curls in my stomach and I stare down at my hands.

"I guess you're right. I just..."

"Storm's been spiraling, kid. He needs a fresh start, a place he can move on from Joey and grow into his potential. I was hoping that was going to be here, that we'd keep building out our core of guys around him, that he'd be the center of the next stage after Lake and Riggs and Knox and Colt retire."

Because he's younger than the veterans.

Because he's going to be in the league for years yet.

"But if he continues as he's going, he won't have potential to grow into. He's going to flame out and—" My brother pushes to his feet, shoves his hand through his hair, and sighs heavily. "I can't help him here."

"I know."

I was right.

I haven't seen Storm since that night at the hospital—or not at any of the Game Nights or dinners or even at Riggs and Ella's baby shower. He's skipped out on team events, on charity functions. Hell, I've barely even seen him at the arena.

He plays and he practices and he works out. That's it.

And now he's leaving the team for good.

"The Harrisburg Hawks were the best choice," Damon says. "They want to build the roster around him, and in a few seasons they're going to give us a run for our money."

Moving closer, I nudge at his arm until he lifts it and wraps it around me. "I know you care about him, that you and Joey both do. So I know you've done what you think is best."

He sighs, kisses the top of my head. "Glad to have your approval, kid."

Light words, but I don't miss the relief in his voice.

Relief *I've* given him.

Yeah, I'm pretty damned cool...and pretty damned sure I'm not broken.

That I wasn't *ever* broken. Not really.

And the man standing across the kitchen, where he and Blake are whipping up some delicious confection for dessert, helped showed me that.

Same as I showed him right back.

"Damn right you are," I tell Damon. "Otherwise I'd make you come back and help with the class party next week."

"Party?" he mutters. "They're in seventh grade. Aren't they a little old for that?"

"Too old for a donut party for acing their tests? Never."

His lips twitch. "Donuts don't sound too bad."

"We're also doing Minute to Win It games. They say you're going down."

"I won't be going down," he mutters. "Because I won't be going *in*."

"You forget that I know your schedule."

"You forget that *I'm* your big brother and can still give you wedgies."

"Joey!" I call from where she's holding Lake and Nova's adorable little girl, bouncing her lightly on one knee.

"Yeah?" she calls back.

"Your husband is being mean to me!"

She grins. "Tell your brother that since he knocked me up, he'd better behave himself."

Gasping, I turn to Damon. "You said you guys were going to wait until the timing was right."

A shrug as he hugs me tight. "Turns out I have a kid sister who's damned good at giving advice." He pulls back. "And swimmers that work on the first try."

"Ew." I gag. "No mention of *swimmers* in my presence please."

"Would you like more specific terminology?"

"God no." But I'm laughing and hugging him again and then the news is spilling through the kitchen, congratulations being shared all around.

And I understand why Joey is four months along but they're only just now sharing the news.

They were waiting until Storm wasn't here to be hurt by it.

"I love you guys," I tell her as I hug her tight. "And I'm so happy for you."

"I'm terrified," Joey admits. "And so damned excited." Her expression sobers. "You heard the other news?"

My eyes drift toward Colt. "About Ambrose getting a slap on the wrist?"

A suspension—albeit a long one.

And a fine—yup. A *fine*.

But no criminal charges.

She scowls. "Yup. It's bullshit but it's also not surprising, I suppose."

"I think we both know that wheels of justice don't always work like they should."

Joey went through her own nightmare...and the difficulties that came from securing a fair resolution afterward. "Unfortunately, that's the truth." A sigh. "My only consolation is that I don't think he's going to last long in the league—and that more than one player wants to make his remaining games a misery."

That makes me feel better. Slightly.

"There is that."

She nods toward Colt. "He okay with it?"

I shrug. "He's had bigger fish to fry."

Supporting Blake in his move, getting new doctors set up and caregivers and insurance and prescriptions and modifying the house so his brother can be as independent and comfortable as possible.

And doing all that while Donna—not his mother, because she was never truly that—fought him and Blake every step of the way.

But we're here now.

Blake—and I (and Blake's foster kittens)—moved in.

Sara with a new job at the local hospital and taking over my lease.

Donna pouting and licking her self-inflicted wounds, both of her sons having gone no contact.

And best of all...tonight we're celebrating the likelihood that Holly is soon to be on her way out.

Because Blake has a new job—

As a student advocate.

Adrian is killing it in his classes.

But his parents haven't forgotten what the district pulled.

And they have money...money that's now been earmarked for a non-profit to help kids in Blake's and Adrian's situations.

Kids who've been through too much, who have to carry too much on their young shoulders, and who just want to go to school.

Yeah, Holly's quaking in her boots.

It's great.

That pink slip still may be coming my way.

But there are more jobs, more ways to be there for my kids, including via that non-profit.

I'll be okay.

"When are we getting married?" Colt murmurs, his mouth at my ear as he loops an arm around my middle and draws me back against his chest.

"You have to ask me first, buckaroo," I accuse lightly, spinning in the circle of his hold and poking him in the chest.

A chuckle. A sexy smile that has me melting from the inside out.

"What's that look for?" I ask.

A jerk of his chin. "Turn around, starfire."

Spinning, I see the kitchen's emptied out...

"Where'd—?"

But when I look back to Colt, he's not where I left him.

Instead, he's on one knee, holding—

"Oh, my God!" I gasp.

"What do you say, Teach?"

"Why are you holding Hamish?" I blurt.

His mouth quirks. "Because he's holding something for *you*."

He is. Kind of.

Still, the tiny ribbon Colt has secured around Hamish's neck has my heart pounding, my hands going to my mouth.

Because hanging from it is a shining diamond ring.

"Marry me, baby?" he asks.

I'm frozen, tears pouring down my cheeks, completely unable to form words.

He comes to his feet and draws me into his arms, kissing them away. It's...coming home. It's the beauty of a future together. It's the—

"Did she say yes?!"

Laughter bubbles up in me as I turn around and smile at our family. "You haven't given me a chance to."

Blake grins at me, draws the newest member of our family (hopefully) to his side and my heart squeezes when Sara swipes her finger beneath each eye.

She's sweet and lovely and I understand exactly what Blake sees in her.

Now it'll just be a matter of them going the distance...and I think they will.

"That means yes," he calls.

"Does it?" Colt murmurs in my ear.

I look up at my man, see he's freed Hamish from the heavy weight of that diamond around his neck.

Grinning, I touch his cheek. "Yeah, honey, it means yes."

God, the happiness in his eyes undoes me, even though I only get it for a heartbeat before his mouth is on mine and my lids are sliding closed and he's kissing me...

While he slides on the ring.

It's a perfect fit.

And I know it's not by chance.

Because just like the story of Colt and me...

It's fate.

## STORM

I tug at the black tie around my neck, hating the many pairs of eyes on me as I walk down the aisle and sit in the front row of the church.

It's a bright day, sunshine pouring in through the stained glass windows to send rainbows of color scattering this way and that.

Reminding me that Fate has a fucked-up sense of humor.

Norm Harrison was about as far from sunny as a person could get.

He was the brutal violence of lightning storm, the lashing wind of a hurricane, the destruction of an earthquake...

And now he's gone.

Dead.

Right there on his front porch, beer bottle clutched tight even in death, his face screwed up, prepared to yell at anyone who dared tread too close to his lawn.

Well, the last I don't know for certain, since I wasn't here, but I'd bet my life on it.

Because that was my dad.

"About time you showed up."

I go stiff and look at my brother. He's similarly clothed in a dark suit and tie, his face and muscled body almost a mirror of mine—though where my eyes are gray, his are green, and where my hair falls into my eyes with that trademark hockey flow, his is contained, neatly corralled into an appropriate style for church.

"I'm here." I jerk my chin toward the closed casket. "He doesn't deserve even that much."

"Pot meet kettle," Rain mutters. "Since you're doing your best to be exactly like him."

Rage flashes through me in a hot wave, so intense, so all-consuming that I jerk toward him, that I barely remember I'm in a fucking church, that I'm not on the ice where I'll just get five minutes in the box for beating up this asshole.

My brother.

But still an asshole.

Clenching my teeth together, I look forward again, watching as the priest moves to the lectern and begins talking about my father like he wasn't the asshole everyone in this town knew he was.

Cedar Hollow is the quintessential small town located in the foothills of the nearby mountain range. A destination for tourists with its quaint streets and riverfront location—snow in the winter, apples in the fall, tulips in the spring, rafting in the summer—on its surface, it's a great place to grow up.

Except when one's father is Norm Harrison.

"...and now I'd like to welcome anyone who would like to share a few words about Norm to come up."

The silence that follows...well, yup, Fate has great fucking sense of humor.

Rain sighs from next to me and I don't bother to look at him.

There's no way I'm going up to that mic and saying anything that's remotely close to good.

Something he clearly gets, having grown up in that house.

But my brother is the responsible one, the good one—

So, it's no surprise that he pushes to his feet and finds the one story that doesn't make our dad look like the complete and total bastard he was.

"...and that's when we decided a possum didn't make a very good pet," he says, eliciting soft laughter through the room...and leaving out the part where it wasn't *we*—as in, Rain and I—that decided a possum wasn't a good pet.

Nope. That was Norm.

And our father didn't give one fuck that we'd raised Millie from the time she was a baby, that she relied on us, that she *trusted* us...

We had to set her free.

And when she came crying to the back porch, my dad took out his gun and—

Rain drops back into the pew, hands clenched into fists.

I find that I'm doing the same.

Suddenly, my tie is too tight—or maybe it's my throat.

I need to get the fuck out of here.

"...and give you peace, this day and forever more. Amen."

A sudden rush of noise and movement snaps me out of the past and I burst up to my feet, push through the throng of people leaving, rounding the corner of the old building and not stopping until I'm alone, until I can breathe past the lump in the back of my throat.

Movement out of the corner of my eye.

My head shoots up and...

Time stops.

Six years vanish.

I'm that kid on Cedar Hollow beach again, lusting after a girl in a skimpy pink bikini.

"You okay?" Poppy Baker asks softly.

"Great." It's dry, and sharp enough to wound.

And she winces as though I've done exactly that.

Nodding, she turns away, and though I open my mouth to apologize, I find the words don't come.

*Can't* come.

Because a little girl with dark brown hair plaited into neat pigtails skips up to Poppy and takes her hand. She's wearing a simple black dress, tights, and shining black shoes, but I barely register that because her gray eyes—*my* eyes—flick toward me as she asks,

"Mom, can we go get ice cream now?"

---

I hope you enjoyed Colt and Kylie's journey to forever (and Hamish, the coo's, small role in their HEA) :) I can't wait for you to read Storm's story in SMALL TOWN, BIG STORM, the first book in my brand new Cedar Hollow series! **On the rink, they play to win. In Cedar Hollow, they play for keeps.**

CLICK HERE TO READ SMALL TOWN, BIG STORM NOW>

---

And while you're waiting, have you jumped into my BRAND NEW hockey series, the Grizzlies?
If you love hockey players who fall hard and fast for the women they love, pick up book one in the Grizzlies Hockey series, MARRIED TO NUMBER TWENTY-TWO NOW>. **I signed the contract. I just didn't expect her to show up ten years later, ready to cash it in.**

CLICK HERE TO READ MARRIED TO NUMBER TWENTY-TWO NOW>

READ on for a sneak peek below!

## AIDEN

I wake up to a heavy knock on my condo's front door and glare blearily at my phone in the charger.

"Two in the fucking morning," I mutter, grabbing a pillow and clamping it over my ears. "It's two o'clock in the morning on my fucking birthday, and I have to deal with this shit."

This shit being my neighbors.

It's not the first time they've pounded drunk on my door, desperate for their roommate to let them in to what they think is their apartment.

This was sort of funny the first time.

I remember those days, drinking too much, being dumb.

But after the second and the third—where I gained status into the inner circle and a code to the keypad to their apartment door—it was no longer cute.

Now, six months later and countless times of bailing them out, I'm *so* not in the mood.

Especially when it's my fucking birthday.

The knocking cuts off and I think—*pray*—that they've gotten the hint.

But it's approximately two seconds later when it starts up again.

I glance at my phone again, see that really five minutes have passed, making it two-seventeen and officially my birthday.

Some present.

I could try to ignore it—but that just means extending the torture. Sighing, I toss back the blankets and stomp to my apartment door, whipping it open to reveal a slender brunette on my doorstep.

"Ho, mama," she says, gaze taking a slow perusal down my body.

"Who the fuck are you?"

"It's me. Luna."

I stare at her, uncomprehendingly.

"From Rockfield?" she adds.

Recognition begins to dawn. "Luna Maybelle?"

"Yup! That's me." She nods, grinning, and I see it then, the glimpse of my best friend from the childhood rink I grew up playing at come out in her smile. Mischief and life. Joy and hard work.

Summers spent spending every spare moment together— her figure skating, me playing hockey.

But she's not little Luna anymore.

Christ, she's anything but—tall, beautiful, curves for days— and she's staring at me.

Because I'm staring at her.

Fucking hell.

I spur myself into motion.

"Luna! Oh my God!" I pull her into a hug. "What the hell are you doing here?"

"It's your birthday!" She holds up a piece of paper that looks faintly familiar. "And, well, it's mine too, remember?"

That's right.

We have the same birthday.

"We're both twenty-five, single, and—"

My eyes narrow in on the paper. It's crumpled and stained, as though it's years old.

A purple and pink swirl decorates the edges and suddenly I remember her painstakingly drawing it as we sat side-by-side at one of the high top tables of the ice rink, waiting for the Zamboni to finish cutting the ice.

Her brow had been furrowed. Her movements carefully controlled.

And I had been obsessing over how pink her lips were and

what her butt looked like in her skating dress, so much so that I barely remember what we'd been drawing.

No, I think hard, grabbing on to those memories, not what we'd been *drawing*.

The contract we'd put together.

The contract my hormonal twelve-year-old self had signed.

With a sparkly pink colored pencil.

A giant boulder settles in my stomach, but before I can snap myself out of the horror of those memories, she shoves the paper in my hands then throws her arms around my neck.

"We're getting married!"

CLICK HERE TO READ MARRIED TO NUMBER TWENTY-TWO NOW>

# SIERRA HOCKEY

Snowed
Over the Line
Caught from Behind
The Big Skate
On the Fly
Attacking the Zone

Hate missing Elise's new releases? Love contests, exclusive excerpts and giveaways?
Then signup for Elise's newsletter here!

www.elisefaber.com/newsletter

And join Elise's fan group, the Fabinators (https://www.facebook.com/groups/fabinators) for insider information, sneak peaks at new releases, and fun freebies! Hope to see you there!

If you enjoy my series, considering supporting me on PATREON! Get access to early releases, bonus content, character art, audiobooks, special edition covers, swag, and much more!

CLICK HERE TO SUPPORT ME>

I so appreciate your help in spreading the word about my books, including sharing with friends! Please leave a review on your favorite book site!

## ALSO BY ELISE FABER

***Breakers Hockey (all stand alone)***

Broken

Boldly

Breathless

Ballsy

Bewitched

Blowout

Breathe

Blazed

### Sierra Hockey Series

Over the Line

Caught from Behind

The Big Skate

On the Fly

### Eagles Hockey Series (all stand alone)

Broken Laces

Lace 'em Up

Knotted Laces

Loaded Laces

Lucky Laces

### Oak Ridge Vineyards

Bottles & Blades

Beauty & the Boardroom

The Bachelor & the Break-in

### Rush Hockey Trilogy #1

Big Puck Energy

Filthy Puckboy

So Pucking Over It

### *Rush Hockey Trilogy #2*

Love, Pucks, and Other Stories

All's Fair in Pucks and War

No Pucks Lost Between Us

### *Rush Hockey Novellas*

Puck and Make Up

### *Billionaire's Club* (**all stand alone**)

Bad Night Stand

Bad Breakup

Bad Husband

Bad Hookup

Bad Divorce

Bad Fiancé

Bad Boyfriend

Bad Blind Date

Bad Wedding

Bad Engagement

Bad Bridesmaid

Bad Swipe

Bad Girlfriend

Bad Best Friend

Bad Rebound

Bad Romance

Bad Business

Bad Billionaire's Quickies

### *Love, Action, Camera (all stand alone)*

Dotted Line

Action Shot

Close-Up

End Scene

Meet Cute

### *Love After Midnight* **(all stand alone)**

Rum And Notes

Virgin Daiquiri

On The Rocks

Sex On The Seats

### *Life Sucks Series*

Train Wreck

Hot Mess

Dumpster Fire

Clusterf*@k

FUBAR

Perfect Storm

Free Fall

Lost Cause

### *Roosevelt Ranch Series* **(all stand alone, series complete)**

Disaster at Roosevelt Ranch

Heartbreak at Roosevelt Ranch

Collision at Roosevelt Ranch

Regret at Roosevelt Ranch

Desire at Roosevelt Ranch

## *Phoenix Series* (read in order)

Phoenix Rising

Dark Phoenix

Phoenix Freed

## *Phoenix: LexTal Chronicles* (rereleasing soon, stand alone, Phoenix world)

From Ashes

In Flames

To Smoke

## *KTS Series (all stand alone, series complete)*

Riding The Edge

Crossing The Line

Leveling The Field

Scorching The Earth

## *Cocky Heroes World*

Tattooed Troublemaker

# ABOUT THE AUTHOR

*USA Today bestselling author*, Elise Faber, loves chocolate, Star Wars, Harry Potter, and hockey (the order depending on the day and how well her team -- the Sharks! -- are playing). She and her husband also play as much hockey as they can squeeze into their schedules, so much so that their typical date night is spent on the ice. Elise is the mom to two exuberant boys and lives in Northern California. Connect with her in her Facebook group, the Fabinators or find more information about her books at www.elisefaber.com.

facebook.com/elisefaberauthor

amazon.com/author/elisefaber

bookbub.com/profile/elise-faber

instagram.com/elisefaber

tiktok.com/@elisefaberauthor

goodreads.com/elisefaber